# the girl at the door

# the girl at the door

# veronica raimo

Translated from the Italian by
Stash Luczkiw

Black Cat
*New York*

First published in Italy in 2018 by Mondadori Libri S.p.A.

*Published simultaneously in Canada*
*Printed in the United States of America*

First Grove Atlantic edition: October 2019

This book was set in 12-pt. Minion Pro by Alpha Design & Composition of
Pittsfield, NH

ISBN 978-0-8021-4734-9
eISBN 978-0-8021-4735-6

Black Cat
an imprint of Grove Atlantic
154 West 14th Street
New York, NY 10011

Distributed by Publishers Group West

groveatlantic.com

19 20 21 22    10 9 8 7 6 5 4 3 2 1

*For H.*

"Go home and practice your wooing," I said. "Go on. Go away. Take your Schubert with you. Come again when you can do better."

J. M. Coetzee, *Summertime*

# Her

I was in my sixth month when the girl came knocking.

I'd gotten used to visits at home, almost as if I were sick. In a certain sense I was, a languid infirmity that had me spending the days doing nothing. The doctors prescribed a lot of rest. The challenge was to find new ways of resting.

People were always coming to see me. I'd learned how to receive them. People passed by to ask me how I was, give me advice, and bring me books on motherhood with covers so ugly I didn't know where to hide them. If they didn't bring me books, they came with something to eat. At times it was something potentially toxic, so along with their kindness came a heartfelt self-reproach: "How stupid of me! Tiramisu . . . raw eggs! How could I not have thought about it!"

The girl came empty-handed. Standing on the threshold, her hair down, her jeans tight, just the way I used to wear them before the visitors came to replenish my stock of maternity pants. I was constantly hiding stuff.

"Are you the professor's wife?" the girl asked me.

"Girlfriend, um . . . partner," I specified, even though it embarrassed me to use that term. It felt like I was putting on airs.

"I have to speak to you," she said.

The girl made herself comfortable on the sofa, her empty hands resting on her lap. More than resting, anchored: fingers tensed and knuckles rising white above the fabric of her jeans. Two bones stuck out from the points of her shoulders, two pins lodged in her skin. I sat down slowly on the sofa. My belly suddenly seemed out of place to me, a graceless and garish form I tried to conceal with my hands, which were also more swollen than usual from so much rest—giant hands, fused to my belly in a single mass, florid and vital. Hiding things again. Fortunately, the skeleton on the sofa didn't seem to notice. Her eyes scoured the inside of the house, not suspiciously, but in a sensually empty manner, waiting to fill themselves up.

Neither I nor my boyfriend—the professor, as the girl called him—had been very good at decorating the house. He had been living there longer than I had, but my arrival hadn't changed much. It wasn't a female presence that was missing. Or maybe it was, but surely not mine. I was never interested in furnishings. I don't even know the names of objects; or rather, I know the names, but not what they refer to—words that should evoke something but for me remain merely words:

"valance," "wainscot," "credenza." Anyway, it wasn't an ugly home. When people came to see me, they always complimented it, and they seemed sincere. I know that's what people always do. I guess they have to say something, but I did think the house was welcoming. At least I felt welcome there, even if I'd never done anything to give it more warmth, make it more familiar, more personal. I took it just as it was, as did my boyfriend when it was assigned to him—freshly cleaned—by the university. The walls were painted white, the furniture spartan but comfortable, an armchair for reading, a study where he worked. It was a house where I managed to rest well.

Every once in a while he said to me, "You should buy some knickknacks." But even that was nothing but a word. What does a knickknack look like?

When he sent me the photos of the house to entice me to join him, I made the same assessment as other people. "Looks really cute." "You'll like it," he kept saying. And in fact, I did like it. So the girl could look around all she wanted, but she wouldn't find anything strange to feed her gaze.

"Would you like some tea?" I asked her.

It had become my specialty. I spent a lot of time choosing tea at the market and a lot of time preparing it. Before I got pregnant, it had never occurred to me to think of tea as a possible beverage. Or maybe before moving here. Now it's not just a beverage but an experience, an intellectual emptying, another act of abandonment to accompany my state of infirmity. The Miden market was full of tisanes, loose dried herbs sniffed from burlap bags or metal containers, aromatic teas rich in history, teas that spoke of distant places. I gave myself up docilely to an idea of exoticism that had never seduced me before—but if maternity manuals were the alternative, then submission was all right by me.

"Whatever," the girl said.

I prepared the tea, placed it on the table between us.

"Is green jasmine okay?" I asked her.

"Fine," she said.

"Sugar?"

"Okay."

The girl's brusque manner was beginning to irritate me. It wasn't up to me to explain to her how much life history could be hidden in a cup of tea. Maybe it was her youth that kept her from being contaminated by all that had come before her. And yet she wasn't much younger than I was, even though the gap had opened more substantially as soon as I'd become the professor's girlfriend, or once my womb had borne proof that history existed. But the girl, despite her dismissive comments about the tea, had come to talk about the past.

"I was a student of the professor's," she said to me.

"Okay," I responded to show I could keep up.

"Has he ever spoken about me?"

"Frankly, I don't know. You're not the *only* girl to have been his student."

"I was more than that," she explained.

It was clear what she wanted to tell me. I pretended not to understand.

"The professor and I had a thing," she continued.

We've all had things, I wanted to say. No. Unfortunately, that's not true. I thought of that reply many minutes later, and the mere fact that I didn't think of it quickly enough made it seem particularly brilliant. I spent a few seconds meditating on the girl's words without saying anything. Her tone seemed to suggest exactly that suspended atmosphere, and for lack of a quick retort, I followed her lead.

"Is there a reason I should know this?" I asked.

"Yes," she said. "That's what I'm here for."

My boyfriend and I had met fourteen months earlier in Miden. I was on vacation, and he had moved here some time before that. We were both from the same country. We spent two weeks together. It was love at first sight, or perhaps it was the complicity of two kids a little off balance in a foreign land, even though that may be a romantic way of putting it, considering that he had already been living in Miden for a while, with the prospect of a solid future and his schedule already planned for the new academic year. I could have sincerely claimed culture shock, as I really was a tourist, with no goal at the time and nothing to do either in Miden or elsewhere. So as we were toking up in a tent under the starry sky, it was more the last drops of his vacation we were sharing than the tension of heading into the unknown. And yet, I had cried on one of those nights, my cheeks wet with tears as he spoke of all we could have been. He knew I had nothing to lose, because I had almost nothing. Or at least that's what I liked to think back then. I liked reciting the part. My studies were finished, and all I had were emails from friends who had already left home: I lived in a country you could only leave. Everyone was bailing out. Whoever stayed was infectious. Every day the papers were talking about the Crash, counting emigrants like evacuees, fencing in the survivors. It seemed as if natural disasters were in a period of remission: no earthquakes, hurricanes, or floods. There were no parasites defoliating the trees, no heat waves cracking the parched earth. All they talked about was us, and it made little difference whether we were fifteen or forty. They asked us to have faith. "The worst is over," the politicians said, and then sent their children and money to the other side of the world. The truth is, the worst couldn't be over, because it had never really come. As long as we were children, we would remain children, our mothers and fathers would take care of us. Once I got back home, when I looked at the photos of Miden again, I was convinced that I could see the possibility of life in our idiotic gazes under the Milky Way. And so I left, too. I moved to Miden, trusting that gaze, in which someone—myself, not long after—would have seen nothing more than pot-addled eyes.

I poured some more water in my still-full cup.

"The professor raped me," the girl said.

I have no idea what it means to desire a child. I don't think I desired one; when I found out I was pregnant, that sort of thought had already lost importance. He was there, like I was there. We existed together. The feeling was stronger than desire.

When I moved to Miden, my boyfriend and I made love every day, several times a day, without protection, as they say, since it was clear that our encounter was based on recklessness. Our idiotic gazes under the starry sky were also contemplating the creation of new living beings. Caution and fear belonged to the country we had left. Down there, people died of protection. They died because they held back. Because they were depressed. Because they were afraid. Down there, no one seemed capable of procreating. But we were, we who had gone away, yes, without a second thought. Miden was full of babies.

I looked at the girl. Her skinniness looked threatening, the stripped carcass of an animal come to wreak havoc at home.

"When?" I asked, as if the most important thing were to establish a convincing chronology. But in some ways, it was truly important.

"It happened more than once," she said. "In a certain sense, *always*, all throughout our affair."

"I meant how long ago," I specified.

"Two years ago."

"Would you like some more tea?"

"My cup is full."

I didn't have a great appreciation for music. When I was at home, it never occurred to me to put on an album. Here, visitors never brought me CDs. My boyfriend tried to educate me, but I was too scattered, I couldn't remember the names of the pieces. So when I got up to put on some music, I didn't know what to choose. I was afraid the girl would judge me for a poor choice. She had the air of someone more tuned in to these things than I was. But she was simply stunned that I'd gotten the idea to put on some music. Maybe that's all I was really looking for. Her dismay. I was so incapable of making a good impression that I chose a best hits of the nineties.

"Why have you come to tell me now?" I asked. "I didn't even know him two years ago."

The girl's gaze finally filled up with something; I believe "scorn" is the best word to define it. Even her body seemed more vigorous. She swayed her head back and forth as if it had accrued a weight she couldn't balance.

"Because he was never punished," she responded.

"Did you report him?" I asked.

"No. I couldn't."

"Why not?"

"Because I didn't know then. Now I know."

The girl's fingers didn't even graze the cup I'd placed in front of her. That had been my only kind gesture up until then. The cup alone cost more than her shoes.

"What is it that you now know?" I asked.

"That I was subjected to violence."

# Him

I saved her panties for months. She liked to come to my place and go home without panties. I had a drawerful of them. Then one day when I opened the drawer, I was nauseated. The obscene odor no longer had anything to do with her. In any case I'd long lost her scent, and it was never that good. But the rest of her . . . Her tits, her ass, her legs. I still dreamt about the rest of her. I dreamt about her while I was banging my girlfriend, when I put my hand over her mouth so as to not hear her groan, because I wanted to hear the other girl's groans. In my head, I mean. And then the bitch showed up at my place one day with that absurd letter from the Commission. And my girlfriend even sat there and listened to her. "What the fuck," I said to her. "We both left our own country because we wanted to be free, and you take this shit seriously?" "These are the consequences of freedom," she said to me. She'd started talking like this after she moved to Miden. She spoke in slogans. Or she kept quiet. Either totally emphatic or mute, depressed or hysterical. Even the pregnancy. One day she'd talk about the man he would become, the next day about the toad in her belly. It's not that she was much different when I met her, but she'd always been cheerful, even when she cried. We'd make love and she'd cry. I remember one time when we were camping out, just the two of us on the beach, we were stoned, and she said to me, "Where am I going? I have nothing! Nothing!" her head sunk, crying. But it was as if she were laughing. She was like a baby you needed to hug and console. I said to her, "What does it matter? You have nothing. Good for you. That way you have nothing to throw away." I told her stupid shit like that.

She's convinced that I was the one who asked her to move to Miden. Maybe that's true. That is, I might have said something when we met. She was on vacation and kept carrying on with that same old tune, "I have nothing." So I said, "You have me!" And I believed it. She was beautiful, with her big eyes full of fear, and it was moving the way she looked at me. The long flower-print skirts—I didn't think they made them anymore, maybe they were her mother's or grandmother's, all frayed at the hem from dragging across the ground. At times when she got on top of me, she would keep the skirt on, her tits in the wind, her necklace bouncing from one nipple to the other, her hair tousled, and I remember the filthy hem of that skirt was a bit gross. It swept over the floor day after day. Sure, I admit

I'm someone who saves panties. But that hem still grossed me out a little. So I don't know if it was me who asked her to move. We wrote to each other after she left. I looked at her on the computer screen, and she still had those eyes. What could I say? Come here, I told her. I let her see my place. I read the statistics to her. In Miden they're obsessed with those things because it's at the top of all the rankings. First place for: Quality of life. Trust in the future. Social equality. Human rights. Professional satisfaction. Women's freedom. If you take the sum of all those factors, bingo! What comes out is the thing you're looking for: first place for Happiness.

If I went by statistics, I was a perfectly happy and integrated man of Miden. I had a good-paying job that corresponded to my education and my ambition, with a house made available to me by the university and lots of free time to continue my research and play sports. They even gave me a free pass to the pool. I developed enviable shoulders.

Then the girl showed up with a letter from the Commission. An accusation of sexual assault. My girlfriend looked at her belly and said to me, "I have to think of him." What the hell does he have to do with it? "Do you know what I'm risking?" I yelled at her. And she, as placid as she had learned to be, "Do *you* know what *I'm* risking?" "No," I said to her, "tell me what it is you're risking." "I risk being a rapist's girlfriend." I would have liked to say, Do you remember inside the tent? With your long fucking skirts, bawling nonstop, saying I don't know what to do, I don't know what to do! Like a three-year-old girl. And now suddenly I find this cool, calm woman, as serene as a Buddha, her legs crossed under her prodigious belly, using phrases like "rapist's girlfriend." In the Commission letter they didn't use the word "rapist." There were only mythical figures in that letter. I was the Perpetrator, the one who perpetrated violence. The girl was subjected to it; she was the Subject. The violence is a dodge ball flying at her that she can't manage to dodge, but then two years later she realizes she's covered in bruises. Where were the bruises before? She didn't even know she could get out of the way.

# Her

When I found out I was pregnant, the sky was white.

The sky is always white in Miden, which makes it hard to give memory a background. But the light changes. That day the light was ugly. There were whole mornings that had trouble impressing themselves on my memory; what was left was only the feeling of that absence, the border between day and night crumbling. I'd spoken with someone at the market, but what did we say to each other? Were there any fish with eyes more alive than usual? A pumpkin I would have liked to buy? I no longer remembered anything.

But the girl wasn't talking about repressed memories. What a shame. Because it had become one of my favorite subjects since I arrived in Miden. I wrote many emails about what I was repressing. My friends wrote me impassioned platitudes about how important it is to burn bridges with the past. It was a continual severing of ties, as if we all had a particularly wild and noteworthy past. I get the impression that you can deal with all sorts of conversations by bringing up the idea of clean breaks. You never get anywhere, so you can go on like that for a while, which gives me all the time I need to put the water on the burner for another cup of tea. The fact is that the girl wasn't interested in talking about repressed memories, and she hadn't even taken a sip of her tea.

"How did you find out?" I asked the girl.

"I understood," she responded.

"Okay. How did you come to understand?"

"Thanks to the Commission."

Miden is organized by Commissions. Many scholars come here to analyze the workings of the Commissions. It had started with talk about politics from the ground up, telluric thrusts pressing against the bowels of the earth. This was after the Crash, which, like every Crash, seemed to have come from dizzying heights. My boyfriend hadn't participated in the creation of the Commissions, he moved here later, "but you can still breathe that air," he wrote me in an email. There have been many airs I still haven't had time to breathe, other airs that disperse and consume themselves as I try to write this. When I arrived in Miden, the Commissions already existed, and outside the Commissions there was nothing. If you're a citizen of Miden, you're a member of a Commission. If you don't want to choose one, then one will be

assigned to you. I belong to Organic Pesticides. When scholars come to Miden to analyze how the Commissions work,
they breathe what's left of the air that preceded them and
they go back home with the same disappointed admission:
"It's a mechanism that can only work in a small community."
The inhabitants of Miden are convinced that the reason lies
rather in their DNA—a particularly virtuous and creative
genetic structure. They don't know how to explain it any
other way. The Crash had brought whole countries to their
knees, whereas Miden emerged from the deep waters with
the splendor of a Venus. When I was thinking about writing
an article comparing various approaches to the Crash, the
director of the department where my boyfriend worked said,
"We didn't roll up our sleeves. We chose to put on a new
dress, more beautiful, without any stains." The inhabitants of
Miden like to speak in images. Poetic inspiration is another
characteristic of their DNA that they like to promote. At
dinner there's always someone who brings up the evolution of
their stock from the time their ancestors recited sagas. They
feel like descendants of the Myth, like the gods are still there,
watching them excitedly from the white sky. I see no difference between the scholars' conclusion and a purely genetic
explanation. The Commissions work in a small community,
and Miden is a small community, one so jealous of its own
DNA that outsiders like me are welcomed enthusiastically,

as long as they don't go beyond the limits decided by the Welcome Commission. I never wrote that article about the Crash, or any other. Since I've been in Miden, I've written only emails; the poetic inspiration has yet to contaminate my DNA, even though the emails were quite pretentious.

# Him

Having an affair with a student is never a good idea. There's a reason why it's always discouraged. In my defense I can say that I was a young professor—or, to put it more pathetically, a professor still cutting his teeth. Moreover, in Miden, a foreign land, I needed warmth. To that I can add other, more convincing extenuating circumstances. I taught philosophy at the Art Academy. My female students enjoyed the subject. They were convinced that inserting two or three concepts with a philosophical flavor into their artist statements made their inconclusive discourses more interesting. I believe that my role within the Academy was to be someone who spat out maxims to be recycled in statements. Why were there so many more women than men? I don't know. In one class, for example, there were only three males. Otherwise there was a series of girls who listened to me with interest. Okay, I fucked one of them. It was statistically almost impossible not to, never mind the warmth. But that wasn't the real mistake; the real mistake was to come to my senses and leave her. Once you start something that's wrong, you might as well do it to the end. These sudden assumptions of responsibility are farcical, and it's right to pay the consequences. But I thought I had paid them, because I missed the girl very much. In fact, I held on to her panties.

She dropped my course, but I kept running into her at the Academy. She wouldn't say hi; she would turn the other way. She'll get over it, I told myself. In the meantime, I kept dreaming of her. It didn't occur to me that maybe I wouldn't get over it. I hadn't realized I was in love with the girl until I met my girlfriend and fell in love with her. I don't know why the idea of loving two people at the same time seemed more appealing than one at a time. And I hadn't been in love with my girlfriend before realizing I was in love with the girl. All this would be inexplicable in front of the Commission. Or at least it wouldn't be a very valid argument. In any case, yes, I'd done everything the letter said I'd done. Or rather, *we* had, because it takes two. One time, there were even three of us, the girl and another girl. Never any orgies, but that might have been better at this point. At least I'd have witnesses.

# Her

The girl handed me a letter from the Commission and crossed her legs, as if the gesture had finally conferred upon her the status of an adult. She raised her cup, drinking her first sip of lukewarm tea.

"Please, take your time reading it," she said.

"Now?" I asked, suddenly feeling accused.

"Yes," she confirmed.

"I don't know if I'll be able to understand everything—"

"There's the version in the international language," she interrupted me carefully.

I turned off the music and went into my room to read. The girl watched me go and gestured with her head in a way that could have signaled assent or compassion.

The letter was three pages long.

My boyfriend and I never had any problems talking about

sex. In the beginning of our relationship, that was part of the
excitement. I was more talkative than he was, though I tended to
alter my voice. I either spoke in a falsetto, like a twelve-year-old,
or with a hoarse voice. Not that we said anything special. I would
tell him about past experiences, more or less true, to make myself more slutty. Or I'd pretend it was my first time, or ask him
to block my arms, blindfold me, or come in my face, stuff like
that. He even wanted me to pretend I was one of his students.
"So, what is it that you mean by numen?" he'd say, and I would
look at him like I was totally vapid, and he'd play the part of the
strict and perverted professor. He would slap my ass, punish
me. He would sodomize me with some pseudo-didactic object.
I know, when you're recounting the story, it seems ridiculous
that someone can get turned on by that stuff, but it worked. So
I wasn't surprised to read the list of things my boyfriend and
the girl had practiced, which the Commission drafted. I don't
deny that I was disturbed to read the details, not so much because they were about my boyfriend fucking another woman,
as much as they were the same as our fucks. The only difference
was, she didn't need to pretend that she was a student, since she
was. My boyfriend was called "the Perpetrator" and the girl
"the Subject." On the last page of the letter, the list ended and a
diagnosis appeared. TRAUMA no. 215.

    In Miden there was an apposite Commission created ex-
pressly to evaluate the pertinence of a determined trauma,
and it was subdivided into subcommissions according to the

clinical scope. The exam for becoming a fully fledged citizen of Miden also included a deeper knowledge of the Traumatic Code. I hadn't yet begun to study for the exam, as I still had more than a year before the cutoff date. So, in all honesty, I had no idea what TRAUMA no. 215 was.

When I came back to the living room, the girl had gotten up and was wandering around, her cup in her hand. She stopped in front of a photo of me and my boyfriend taken during the summer we met. I don't usually hang photos, but that one was particularly beautiful. Or rather, that's what you're led to believe when you come out well in a photo.

"Is that you?" the girl asked, as if twenty years had passed since the picture was taken.

"Yes," I answered. "I had longer hair."

She stood there staring at it, nodding her head, almost as if she wanted to ascertain my degree of self-indulgence.

"Seeing a photo of the professor makes me uncomfortable," she said.

"You're in his home," I pointed out.

I went back to sit, with the hope that she would follow suit.

"Listen," I said to her, "I'm starting to feel uncomfortable too. I'll confess, reading that letter was not pleasant—"

"Yes, but it was necessary . . ."

"Why?"

"You're one of the witnesses."

# Him

My girlfriend was called as a witness. So there was no need for orgies, since they had already gathered enough people to give their testimony. Five colleagues—a man and four women. And five people dear to me, classified on the basis of their degree of proximity and sharing with respect to yours truly according to the parameters of the Commission: 1) sentimental involvement, 2) frequency of meeting, 3) affinities of interest, 4) generational comparability, and 5) belonging to the same Commission (I was in Organic Pesticides, just like my girlfriend; it made us laugh, so we decided to join together). The witnesses were supposed to answer questions about my life in Miden, my relationship skills, my vision of the world. Their task wasn't to express an opinion about my guilt as much as to furnish an emotional and behavioral framework of me as a person in order to enable the members of the Commission to draft a verdict. I had been welcomed into a community, but the point was this: Was I still worthy enough to participate? In Miden there are no unworthy citizens. If I were judged guilty, I would be banished. The germ of violence nesting in me could compromise the social fabric. It worked a little like vaccines; if not for herd immunity, we would all be in danger. A Perpetrator must be distanced to prevent other flare-ups, the fresh outbreak of a previously vanquished disease.

I'd been prohibited from going near the girl, from speaking to her. I could only come face-to-face with the witnesses, and they were required to report any attempt to taint their impartial judgment. Under those conditions, having a chat wasn't exactly a pleasure. The saddest thing when looking at that list of people was to realize that I didn't have a single friend in Miden. Or maybe not: even sadder was having such infantile thoughts. One of the reasons I left my country was because of the people who talked that way. At night they would go out with a few friends, get obliterated; then, the morning after, they'd brood about their shitty lives: "I don't have a single friend." They'd sometimes have the thought that same night, looking at everyone else with the exhausted air of someone who already has a bag packed to go. Some of them really did have them packed. Not me. I packed only when I was about to leave.

In any case, none of those witnesses made me think of friendship. I'm not a difficult person, not a snob. I can bond with anyone, I have fun, get bored, I do what I need to do, but friendship is something else. My best friend, together with my previous girlfriend, left my country two months before I did. That is, by the time they left, she was technically no longer my girlfriend, but a week earlier she had been. A week earlier we'd been at my place, she with her head on my lap and an expression of terror on her face: "I feel lonely here. I have no one." And me: "What do you mean you have no one? I'm here." Who knows how I get into these situations. Likewise with my current girlfriend. I must have some sort of last-chance fascination.

# Her

The Commission had prepared a questionnaire about my relationship with my boyfriend. The girl had asked only that I be sincere, and she gave me the email address of the director of the Commission in case I had any questions for her.

"If you like," she said with sudden kindness, "I'll tell her to come see you."

I knew the director. My boyfriend had introduced me to her shortly after I'd moved. In the beginning he was rather worried about my poor social skills. Or maybe he was just channeling everyone else's fear. In Miden, nobody had anything against two hearts sharing the same hearth—or even one solitary heart. And yet you felt the pressure of a greater, more generous idyll: the Miden Dream, which claimed a tribute of universal love from you. But I never joined any of the spontaneous groups they organized to spend free time together. Even my boyfriend belonged to only two groups, and the pool group was not his choice, since the university had given him a free pass. The other was the wine lovers' group. I would have gone too, but, for one thing, I didn't want to seem so attached to him, and for another, the wine in Miden was undrinkable. There were also tea lovers, and every morning I woke up with the sincere intention of signing up. But I lacked a certain ease. I still spoke the international language; it seemed a bit senseless to enter a circle of enthusiasts and not be able to catch the nuances and secrets.

In any case, my boyfriend introduced me to the director "before anyone knew better." This has become an overused expression in my life since the girl's visit. From that day on, it seemed that everyone knew better. I wouldn't say that the director and I had become friends, but we did do some activities together. On Thursdays, for example, we went to the movies. Neither of us had particularly brilliant commentary on the movies we saw, so we just kept repeating how pleasant it was to have that weekly date, to remember with insincere nostalgia the time of projectionists, and once in a while to complain about someone whispering during the movie. One afternoon we even went to the steam bath. We discreetly examined each other's nude bodies. Mine was essentially hairless apart from my pussy; hers was the exact opposite. Then we lay down on the couches at the entry, reading our horoscopes aloud from the gossip magazines and trying to amuse ourselves. I didn't catch the funny bits, because I only understood half of what was being read, so I wound up laughing more than I should have.

After missing our appointment two Thursdays in a row, we stopped seeing each other. If we happened to meet on the street, we reassured each other that we would call soon. Neither of us did. Many of my relationships in Miden were like that. I guess a lot of relationships any place in the world are like that. The only inconvenience is that in Miden, you often meet people by chance.

That said, there was no reason to send an email to the director, because the questionnaire was very simple, too simple. I would have liked some more insidious questions, to pause a few seconds with the pen in my mouth to follow a thought, the way I did when I tried to write. In fact, I was almost offended by such an inane questionnaire. It made me feel like an imbecile. Let's not aggravate a pregnant woman, the questions seemed to suggest. So I thought about writing the director an email. I'd tell her that the sight of her hairy body in the steam bath was disgusting, that I forced myself to look at her because it would have been embarrassing not to. That the idea of her toxins mistakenly attached to my skin revolted me. That the smell of her breath while she was lying next to me reading the horoscope—even though mitigated by the ginger tea they offered us—reeked of rotten cabbage. That if she really wanted to know, I found the memory of that afternoon much more repugnant than the image of the girl taking it up the ass from my boyfriend.

# Him

All the witnesses agreed on one thing: I should never have started that affair. "She was *your student!*" they kept repeating, as if the concept itself should have been enough to deter me. But the affair started, and was finished, so to keep brooding on that point didn't seem like a great idea. And yet, that was exactly what I was supposed to do from the moment I started my meetings with the witnesses, which consisted of sifting through a "real ugly story." That was how my colleague from artistic anatomy, for example, defined it. It was beautiful, too, I pointed out to him, but he shook his head the way you would with a student as thick as he was recidivist, a student you would gladly smack upside the head if it were allowed. My colleague couldn't come to terms with the fact that a philosophy professor could have such a maggot-ridden notion of beauty. For that matter, he couldn't even come to terms with my presence in the

Academy. What point was there in studying philosophy if you wanted to be an artist? It was a more-than-legitimate doubt, so much more that it became my doubt too. Apart from our common vision about the utility of philosophy (which I was never self-indulgent enough to share with him), he and I never really liked each other. It might be in bad taste to mention the Aesop story of the fox and his sour grapes, but I'm sure my colleague was writhing with envy when he found out I'd been fucking the girl. I have my reasons for believing this. He had put himself out like a madman to organize a terrible exhibition for her in a friend's gallery and had obliged all his colleagues to go to it, like a company field trip. Her work barely filled half a room; the other half was occupied by a row of wine glasses and female students eager to doll themselves up in their artsy way. The girl wore a lamé dress that brushed her ass, with a granny cardigan over it. The night of the show, half drunk, my colleague made a move on her. She told me when we were at my place, an hour after the opening, when she finally took off her cardigan and straddled my legs, still wearing that lamé dress. I asked her why she didn't go for it. "He would've fixed you up with another show," I said. She called me an asshole, but she laughed. She said my colleague creeped her out because his Adam's apple was always reddish, like a skinned bollock. She always came out with stuff like that to drive me crazy. So I ordered her to touch it next time and tell me how it felt. First she called me an asshole, then a pervert as she licked my throat and sucked my Adam's apple. It felt weird, like I had a dick under my chin, and she started getting wet on my lap. Fortunately, that anecdote doesn't appear in the list of practices between me and the girl. Maybe she was ashamed. And yet, she had the idea of making a sculpture called *The Skinned Bollock* and offering it to me as a scalp.

# Her

I finished responding to the questionnaire. I had the impression that I could have responded yes or no indifferently to all the questions and still not have lied. When I fucked my boyfriend for the first time, we were so stoned that my sensations that night changed by the second. His face had opened wide above me and appeared monstrous; then a second later I caressed his cheek as if he were a baby. His body had mutated in shape and proportion, his odor was horrifying and irresistible, his randy expression disgusted and excited me. Even his eyes transformed continuously—a stupid gaze, then a deep one, distant and close. I felt like I was fucking a stranger, and I was moved by the familiarity of his embrace. I could smell his rancid alcoholic breath and taste the sensuality of whiskey on his lips. I was frightened by the smack of his hand on my thigh, and I sucked his fingers after they'd reemerged from my pussy.

Did you ever feel abused by your partner? That's what the
Commission asked me. At certain times I wanted nothing
more than to feel abused—by my boyfriend, by life, by enthusiasm, even by the opposite, desperation, alcohol, or drugs,
something that overwhelmed me violently. Or even softly. It
didn't matter how. There are many people who describe their
lives in these terms. They succumb to something. Then they
break away. They damn and regret their damnation. From
the way they describe it, fantastic love always seems be at the
heart of it, a great love affair. There are many TV programs
that recount these stories. The ex-alcoholic with her hair just
fixed by the hairdresser, still a little tousled, who looks at the
TV camera stunned, careful never to blink. Alcohol was her
lover, her demon, her master. Then there's the anorexic, prey
to other demons. And the junkie. And the gambler (a man),
and even the writer who was afraid she would take her own
life because she heard voices. For so little, I thought. At least
she heard voices, felt presences. You can have a chat, I wanted
to tell her. Much better to feel presences than to feel fuck-all.
Anyway, no, I never felt abused by my boyfriend.

# Him

One of the few witnesses to show any comprehension was the swimming instructor. She didn't teach me, just the little kids. She was listed as one of my friends. When I went to the pool, I liked watching her from my lane. From a distance her legs looked very long. She struck an elongated and imposing figure, a sort of muscular statue with a watery sheen, and her hair tucked tight into her light-colored swim cap made her head just as sculptural. But when you got closer, you realized she was much tinier than you'd have expected. She was a giant among the kids because they were small. Even her legs looked shorter; they were still alluring, but they wouldn't make you think of a statue. So I preferred watching her from afar, staring at her thighs as she came out of the water. I've always liked going to the pool, more than to the sea. There were fewer risks in the pool to erode my competitive spirit. And I couldn't care less about catching an octopus with my bare hands. I was into clean and clinical competition, without any heroism. I even liked women in their Olympic one-piece suits more than in floral bikinis. The forms were more defined, the asses, arms, and shoulders a precise geometry of solids. There was nothing romantic in admiring those bodies, and it relaxed me to watch a girl dart by in her lane and pull up to me; I would pass her at the last moment and imagine her little frustration as she touched the pool's edge with her foot to turn and catch up with me again. In the Miden pool there were excellent female swimmers, and I presume they weren't interested in seeing a man with an octopus in his hands. We didn't want to get dirty with sand, smell the pestilential odor of algae, or burn ourselves on the hot pebbles. I've never understood who gets pleasure from nudism, swimming naked in the open sea, being in contact with the elements. To me the most exciting thing is the elimination of all friction, tight suits gliding through the pool's bright blue water. I've never yearned to feel like a fish, but rather to be a perfect laboratory creature, measuring myself against the other creatures, win or lose.

The swimming instructor beat me a couple of times when I challenged her, and during the races I stopped thinking about her size. From the chats we had, she came across as a sympathetic woman. She tried to understand. And to explain. Maybe it was an occupational hazard; there's something intrinsically pedagogic about her because she has to deal with children. Or maybe—I said to myself—she wondered why I hadn't come on to her, since after the affair with the girl, I'd suddenly become known as a womanizer. I've never been a womanizer. I admire beautiful women, like everyone else, but I'm too lazy to put in the effort. I don't like the idea of random hookups. I might have come on to the instructor had we managed to keep our distance: me in my lane and she at the other end of the pool. When I had a band, before Miden, our best song was called "Sidereal Distance." I played the bass. I should have learned more from those years.

The instructor explained to me what it meant to be a girl and take a fancy to a professor. She used that expression "take a fancy to"; she wasn't worried about revealing the shortness of her legs up close, but with her words she made sure to keep a little distance. In any case, no one said anything about love in all those pages written by the Commission, so there's no reason to expect the witnesses to mention it either. All the same, she was warm in her report about "taking a fancy." I don't know if she'd had that experience too, and still felt the effects. Without her saying it outright, her point of view was that it was a mistaken affair from the outset. On that point, I conceded. I stopped trying to justify it and in fact would often bring it up myself: What was in my head? Then I prepared to nod before she could. But what sense was there in accusing myself of violence after all that time?

"Some things need time to process," she told me.

"Okay," I said, "but maybe in two years she'll process something else, and we'll be back to the beginning."

"Then in two years we'll talk about it again."

"It's not like truth can change infinitely."

She paused reflectively.

"I was expecting a more dialectical approach from a philosophy professor," she quipped. "I believe it took centuries to show that the earth wasn't flat."

"That example has nothing to do with it."

"It does, it does . . ."

"That was a scientific demonstration. It wasn't a question of interpretation—"

"Listen, there's no need for scientific demonstration."

"Yes, exactly, but you're the one who brought up the flat earth."

"Who cares about the earth? They might one day discover it's a cube."

"Well, in that case it would be a matter of false truth."

"But we're not talking about the earth!"

"Exactly, we're not talking about the earth!"

"This is about a girl who felt she was raped," she said.

"The point is that two years ago, she didn't *feel* raped."

"She didn't understand. As a child, you don't understand if your father is violent. You figure it out later."

"She wasn't a child, and I wasn't her father."

"You were her professor!"

# Her

I would have liked to call the girl. I was carrying a being in my womb, maybe I should have tried to be more maternal. Maybe I could have explained things to her. I wasn't really an idealist, but I did have my own ideals. She was born in Miden; her father was one of the founders of the Dream. The Crash had barely grazed her, an anomalous migraine that tormented her one morning, only to fade in the afternoon. For me it was different. What are you doing? I would have asked her. Why are you doing it? Should I have allowed myself a little theatrics? Why are you doing this *to us*?

The annoying thing was that the girl didn't seem the least bit interested in my boyfriend. It wasn't a form of revenge for her as a betrayed, disappointed, or frustrated lover. There were no such feminine subtleties. It was all matter of fact. So even my desire to do a little bit of theater—invite her out to lunch at a nice restaurant where she would never have gone, make her feel uneasy, observe her not touching her food the way she didn't touch her tea, and ask, Why are you doing this to us?—would have all been vaguely ridiculous, seeing as how she wasn't doing it to hurt me or him, but just "for herself," as she would have said in that insufferable tone of hers. And she would have fixed that bottomless gaze on me, a gaze I'm sure could have erased my theatrical banquet, the nice restaurant, my hair loose for the occasion, and my glass of red wine (going against the recommendations of my doctor: "If you must, then half a glass of white, not red." As if there really were a difference in the swill that was sold in Miden).

But there was another factor that rendered the question altogether inadequate. It didn't take much concentration for me to understand that my boyfriend had lost the necessary desperation and amazement to fear an attack that could destroy us. There was nothing to destroy. It was a rather calming truth. We weren't fighting against anyone. I like deluding myself that there was a time when it was different. We had worked out our first encounter very well. At times I had the impression that we were constructing a story to tell our children: *And that's how Mom and Dad . . .* We had all the necessary requirements for being credibly in love then. The sea, the tent, the Miden dawn, the sex, and the country we had left behind. Not to mention our emails. We had material for our children, and then some. It was just us two against everyone, we would tell them. There was no reason for them to doubt it.

# Him

The swimming instructor thanked me. I'd opened her mind, she said, with that example of the violent father. Actually, the example was hers, I noted. Who knows where I got this desire to play the sophist just as my whole life was going to shit. Or going to whores, as they say in my country. "Going to whores" was one of the expressions that sparked the most debate in the linguistic exchange meeting I'd attended after moving to Miden. The reactions alternated between hilarity and indignation, often flowing together in a surge of shameful consternation, as when kids first discover that they stink if they don't wash. The meeting's mediator proffered her theory: in the end there should be nothing wrong with going to sex workers as long as they are happy, pay their taxes, and are good company. So an expression like that—I pointed out to her—would be useless. It would be "my life is going for a stroll," more or less. The mediator reflected on that: "Yes, why not? It would be good to get some fresh air."

My swimming instructor was grateful to me because I had given her a way of proposing to the Commission on Relations with Minors that they consider TRAUMA no. 215 in certain cases between parents and children. She wasn't part of that Commission, but there's always a certain pride among the inhabitants of Miden when they manage to venture across Commissions. Some amuse themselves this way to pass the time, constantly looking for good ideas to propose. Then they often discover that someone else has already proposed the same idea. These things happen.

"So the trauma has to come up before the age of eighteen?" I asked.

She looked at me, perplexed. "No. There are no temporal limits."

"So you'll have to find another Commission."

I could see she was disappointed.

"I'm sure you'll find it," I reassured her. "It sounds like a great idea."

# Her

I didn't call the girl. But I decided to write in my diary that day. Maybe they would include it in the trial material. At least I would have some readers. It was a little less frustrating than responding to the questionnaire. I wrote a good diary entry. I was hoping they'd take it into consideration. I was hoping they'd ask me to keep going. However this story wound up, I told myself, there would be someone interested in my version. I even knew a guy at the Publishing Commission. So I started with that little diary entry. I reread it many times and was extremely satisfied. I thought, after the pregnancy I can start smoking again, I can sit in my boyfriend's study while he's at the Academy and try to write. I reread that diary page and thought of myself without a belly, without tea, with whiskey and a cigarette. Pages and pages at my boyfriend's desk. Maybe we would buy a new one. I would choose something at the Miden market that felt more lived-in than the white laminate. A real wooden table. Full of veining. Walnut. Cherry. Oak. As if I knew the difference.

# Him

I saw the girl on the street. I stopped her, thus violating the restraining order.

"We need to talk," I said.

"I really don't think so," she said. "As a matter of fact, you *can't* talk to me."

"Do you realize this is absurd?"

"Do you realize that I was assaulted?"

She spoke as if she wanted spectators. I was the only one on the street; we were outside the Senior Citizens' Garden. Who knows what she was doing there. I never thought that the kids in Miden had grandparents. But if they did have any, they were all there in the garden. I never saw any old people anywhere else. Inside the garden you could see silhouettes dressed in white, filling baskets with cherries. Fruit trees don't grow in Miden, because summer barely lasts a month. I believe workers attached cherries to the trees. In fact, they were fir trees.

"I loved you," I told her.

The girl gathered her hair back with her hands and stood there, her elbows raised in the air. I saw the blond hair under her arms, a scrape from the bike on her elbow, and I was moved. It was cold, but she couldn't wait to go sleeveless. Even to class, she always wore a tank top. On top of it she wore a formless oversized jacket, pieces of cloth that hardly covered her bones underneath. She stood with her elbows suspended, as if waiting for something else. Then she lowered her skinny arms.

"What about now?" she asked.

"Not anymore."

"I loved you too."

We couldn't have found a sadder way of saying it.

# Her

In bed, my boyfriend caressed my belly, keeping his hand there to check if he could feel any movement. I took his hand and slid it farther down. I started masturbating with his hand, and he let me.

"I want to be the girl," I said to him.

"What?" he said.

"Do to me what you did to her."

My boyfriend pulled his hand away.

"What the fuck are you saying?" he shouted, sitting on the bed, looking like he wanted to smack me in the face.

"Yeah," I said. "Let's start with a smack. Did you smack her? The letter from the Commission doesn't say anything about that. It only mentions spanking."

I got up and turned on all fours.

"Don't play crazy," he said.

"I want to know how it feels to be raped," I said.

"I never raped her!" my boyfriend shouted, and got up. Who knows where he thought he was going. He rummaged through his dresser drawer as if looking for his cigarettes, but he never kept them there. It wasn't easy to rummage through an empty drawer.

I stayed there on the bed, on all fours. My belly grazed the mattress.

When I went for walks in Miden, I met a lot of mothers with their newborn children. I saw them bend over the strollers with their backs straight, bent perfectly at a right angle, the way they teach you in yoga. I'd taken a few yoga lessons at the beginning of my pregnancy. The teacher's attention was insufferable: I was pregnant and foreign, and she treated me like a panda. So I stopped. While I was on all fours there on the bed, I looked at myself in the mirror on the wall. Every once in a while we used it to get turned on, even though I don't get very turned on by watching myself fuck. But my boyfriend liked it. He grabbed me by my hair and forced me to watch. I did, but couldn't find anything seductive in my red and swollen face; he evidently could. I took off my nightgown and went back on all fours to look at myself in the mirror. I tried to lengthen my back. My shoulders slouched and my arms had no muscles. I lifted my head to stare at my boyfriend, who was still next to the drawer.

"I want to be the girl," I said again.

"Stop it," he said.

"I'm one of the witnesses. I need to understand."

My boyfriend came up to the bed and pulled my arm out from under me so I'd lose the pose. I fell on my side. I kept looking at myself in the mirror. I was more decent in the fetal position. All you could see was my belly, the mercy and stronghold of those days.

# Him

We went to bed late that night. During dinner my girlfriend poured herself a couple of glasses of wine. I didn't like monitoring her, appealing to common sense. Two glasses of wine, I said to myself. Okay, who cares. But then, after dinner, she insisted on a dash of whiskey. I didn't say anything, I just gave her a look that struck me as eloquent, hence the look of an asshole. Usually those looks elicit the opposite effect from what was intended; in fact, she poured herself an abundant glass of whiskey and drank it down in one gulp as I sat there sipping mine.

"How do you manage to still enjoy things?" she asked me, as if there had been some prelude to that question, as if we'd already discussed it and that was all we ever discussed. But then what was it we were discussing?

We went to bed with our moods spoiled, but I had a desperate need for warmth. I nestled in under the covers with the comforter pulled up to my nose. I just wanted to stay there, next to her, hold her tight, enjoy the warmth of that familiar bed—since I was still able to enjoy things. So I extended a hand to her belly, trying to feel the baby's movements. Usually I don't feel anything, but it relaxes me. It's an exercise in meditation. I close my eyes, I know I'm there, together with both of them. I didn't feel anything.

# Her

My boyfriend lay down beside me, behind me. He hugged me. We stayed like that for a few moments, like two lovers in a mattress commercial. I felt his breath on my neck.

"We could repaint this room," he said.

It must have seemed like a tender way of changing the topic. Usually it's women who come up with these kinds of things, out of the blue, as if they had a whole series of them packed away somewhere: We could go for a trip to the lake. We could go see that funny silent film. We could buy a nice lamp for the living room.

Nothing clashed with the color of the walls. They were white.

"For the baby," he added.

I don't know what kind of color perception a newborn has, but I believe that in this case, to say "for the baby" has a much more extensive meaning. In the mirror in front of us I saw my boyfriend's leg on mine. His tapered and nervous feet always made a great impression in a pair of sandals. There are men who can't pull it off, but he looked great in them.

In the girl's letter to the Commission, there were three practices that involved those feet: my boyfriend had walked on her; she had licked them; he had masturbated her with his foot.

"What color were you thinking of?" I asked.

"Light blue," he said. "Or aquamarine."

Before moving to Miden, I'd lived in different apartments and houses. I lived with other people, students, young workers, dogs at first, then cats. In every place, there was always a room with aquamarine walls. Or, more precisely, each place had a room with some sort of green that the renter at the time described as aquamarine. The variation was baby blue.

"If you walked on me now," I asked, "do you think we could consider it assault?"

My boyfriend kept silent, his breath intensifying on my neck.

"If you walked on my belly," I continued, "could we consider it a form of violence?"

"I should say so," he said. I could feel him straining to keep calm.

"And if I consented?" I asked.

"Then we'd both be idiots," he said.

# Him

I reconsidered my life prior to Miden. Before the girl. Before my girlfriend. I thought about my friends. Our evenings together talking about how we were going to make it big with our music. I thought about my parents. Even about my grandparents. I thought about their old age. I thought about my father's father, his war stories, how he ate a piece of dog shit thinking it was a hunk of dried bread. I thought about how he'd never gathered cherries from a fir tree. There I sought the warmth I needed that night. I didn't find it.

# Her

I've never been walked on by my boyfriend. From among the practices in the letter, that was one we hadn't tried. I wondered how he did it with the girl, who was a wisp. How did he manage not to break her back? How much self-control did he need to exercise in his excitement? How much loving care to choose the right point on which to place his feet without causing damage: a thigh, at the edge of the belly, but not the chest? Or maybe she was turned over with her back facing up, in which case so was her ass, but he couldn't step on her vertebrae without fear of hurting her. Such care was moving, so moving that I would have liked to have my own vertebrae shattered, one after another. But I wasn't like that. I wasn't the one possessed by demons. A glass of whiskey too many to make my boyfriend angry was the extent of my wrath. The spine-snapping demon, the demon that slits your wrists, the demon that comes to stick your head in the oven or wake you at 4:48 a.m. has never deigned to even glance at me.

# Him

I wrote to the girl. I didn't know what the penalty might be. I could have found out if I had read the restraining order, but if I had read the restraining order, I wouldn't have written to the girl. That's what's called rigorous reasoning.

It seemed easier to write a post-love letter, about the kind of love that was lost. We're more used to those feelings, or more expert at them. Or maybe regret just has an interesting density.

I've written love letters too, when I was younger. At university. I stuffed them with quotes, depending on what exam I was preparing for. And I wrote love songs. But in that case there were other elements to consider, the sense of rhythm, which words sounded good.

She answered me:

*I wonder how it would've been if what happened hadn't happened. How it would be now. But it's an impossible thought, because the trauma has by now become a part of my identity. And you would no longer recognize me. I'm no longer who I was.*

*I also wonder how the future will be, if we'll ever see each other again.*

*If you're convicted, you'll have to leave Miden. And I don't think I'll go looking for you. I've thought about this, too: many years from now, when I'm healed. Two adults? Two old people? How would it be then?*

*Don't ever write me again. All this will be part of the trial. Your letter is already in the file.*

She was right, I might never have recognized her. Not because of the trauma. She'd become cunning. I heard every word measured for the Commission, but it was a sincere letter. She wondered how the future would be, but I already saw the future there: she was no longer a girl. As for healing, there didn't seem to be anything to heal.

# Her

That morning, there was sun in Miden, as pale as a Mormon but intense enough to need sunglasses.

I took a walk around the market. I bought a juniper berry tea and aquamarine pajamas for the baby, like the color he'd never see on the walls.

I felt the oppressive desire to smoke, even though I hadn't touched a cigarette since the first day of my pregnancy.

The lady at the tobacco shop had me try the new flavors of herbal cigarettes: hazelnut, elderberry, blueberry. Normal cigarettes are not allowed to be displayed in Miden, and they cost about the same as a dinner out. I asked for a packet. I wasn't sure which Commission the tobacconist belonged to, so I cautiously added, "They're for my boyfriend. He's trying hard, but just can't quit."

She gave me an indulgent smile and slipped into the back to get some cigarettes. As I pulled out money to pay, she said, "But your partner is—"

I nodded without letting her finish the phrase.

"I'm sorry," she said. She cast me an apprehensive glance, as if she herself didn't quite know what to do with her eyes.

"You shouldn't buy him cigarettes," she added.

"It's a complicated situation," I said.

"Of course," she said.

After the tobacconist came all the others. I started wearing sunglasses even when the light was gray. "If you need something . . ." they said without continuing the sentence. I would smile, trying to avoid the start of a conversation. They didn't seem that keen on conversation either. It was all a pantomime of increasingly heartfelt looks and kind gestures. It took me twice as long to do my shopping at the market. There were always those moments of caring ferocity: me standing there with a dazed smile while somebody filled my bag with the best products. I had the feeling that everyone was slowing their movements so as not to destabilize me. But I could tell they were studying me. Someone had seen me smoking, someone had seen me drinking a beer at lunch, someone was wondering about those sunglasses. I started paying more attention to details. I couldn't allow myself to have dirty hair, a shoelace untied, or a stain on my dress, but I knew they would find something anyway. There were those who saw me pale, with a cold, those who noticed that the strap of my shoulder bag was half torn. As for the squalor of my maternity pants, with their elastic band, they kept quiet. They were the ones who'd given them to me. When I went to throw away the garbage, my neighbors were there to say hello, lingering to make sure I didn't put things in the wrong recycling bins. At times I saw them spying on me, looking through the transparent plastic bags for a clue. I don't know what they were expecting to find. Maybe a fetus.

# Him

The girl and I had thought of forming a band together. Ah, we thought of so many things! I hadn't played in years, and she didn't know how to play anything, but her voice wasn't bad. I'm not sure I'd have felt the same if I hadn't gone to bed with her; to be honest, it was the kind of little-girl voice that I couldn't stand in all the young Miden bands, but they all sang that way, and no one had any say in the matter, least of all me. In our best number, though, the girl was silent the whole time and then at the end simulated a sort of orgasm. Her voice disappeared, and there were only groans. It was something almost unlistenable, but I liked to watch her in the role of performer, with her short skirts and those lips making out with the mic. She wanted me to teach her how to play the bass, but she got bored with the practice exercises. The things that bored her were infinite. When we weren't having sex, she always had the air of being delightfully bored. She asked me to show her how to place her hands on the strings, and then she'd send me a photo of her nude with the bass. Those photos never wound up in the Commission files. Evidently the trauma had spared them. She didn't suddenly realize that she'd been forced to take them. No, that's not the correct wording: she didn't suddenly realize that she'd *felt* forced to take them. Everything hinged on that feeling. By now I liked seeing the situation in this manner, as a game. If I removed my antagonism, too, I would have found myself a pathetic character. So I opened the encrypted folder on my computer to look at the girl nude with the bass again. I thought, You were hot, you sent me this stuff, let's enjoy the competition.

There were other photos in the folder, too. Lots of them wound up in the Commission files. I'd taken some of them. But most of them were part of her artistic project. She'd called it *Play and Control*. I was the one who suggested the title. Even that was taken into consideration by the Commission and deemed to be proof of my bad faith, of my manipulative intent. Forcing her to play and exercise control. Of all the girl's artistic projects, I believe it was her best. (You could also comb through this judgment, looking for bad faith, and I have no doubt you would find some. I'm still getting used to the privileges of lying.) I'm not saying it was an original project, not at all. At the Academy's end-of-year exhibit, half of the work was an obsessive repetition of the nude body in almost any form—material, linguistic—at any level of abstraction. And there was always a strange bitterness in those works, the specter of bodies without joy. There was the scent of death, with nothing accidental about it. The girls sought out death in their works; they went into them to commit suicide. A parade of dead bodies. It was like walking through a cemetery. And then I saw them—their live bodies, their febrile eyes, those colored shoes, slight hips, skewed hairdos, the smiles for a compliment, the hands soaring through the air to explain a detail, a finger between their teeth, or a foot crossed over the other. They played coy or got drunk, blathered on, blushed, so fragile and powerful. Yet they set out to kill themselves in their work.

*Play and Control* wasn't like that. The girl was happy in those photos. The girl was happy with me. The trauma wasn't that traumatic. The girl didn't understand that she felt forced to be happy. I'm sure that when the Commission examined the photos, they saw in them what I saw.

# Her

I went to the shore to gather my thoughts. I left home with that noble aim. There's an iconic image of a solitary man standing above the sea; women are usually strolling on the shore. I didn't feel like walking. I sat down in an uncomfortable position on the cold sand and did the breathing exercises the doctors recommended. I shut my eyes and thought of the child. I took deep breaths, thinking of the child. When I opened my eyes, I saw the dark water in front of me and imagined that inside me was a sea just as dark, with a child buried in the darkness. My thoughts were slimy; they wouldn't let themselves be gathered.

I went back home and found an email from my parents. Whenever I got an email from them, I always feared that something bad had happened. I was waiting for news of a catastrophe from one moment to the next. Even a minor catastrophe: a tax audit or a cat hit by a car. But they just wanted to come and see me. My mother attached a photo of a pair of booties she wanted to knit for the baby. I don't know where she got the photos, or to whom those booties belonged. They were set on top of a Formica table in a kitchen I didn't know. I paid less attention to the booties than to the kitchen's particulars. There were objects in every corner, the affective layers of life, notes stuck on the fridge, dishrags, gloves, gadgets for baking, a large quantity of jams, a calendar with recipes, sea-themed watercolors on the walls. The booties were in the foreground, but it was obviously the background my mother was trying to hurt me with. I've never sent her photos of this house. She never came to find me. I had never really invited her. In Miden you need permission to have guests. It's not hard to get, but I never bothered to figure out how. "Well, are you ever going to let us see that belly?" she wrote. She always wrote emails in the plural. I don't know if my father was there next to her while she was writing, or if he only gave his final approval. Or if, more likely, he was in the next room tinkering with something before it even broke. But the email was signed "The Mom and Dad." Their use of the article was endearing; it seemed an attempt to give their affection a weird literary quality. More classical.

Neither the mother nor the father had ever met my boyfriend. I had no doubt that we would all hit it off fantastically once seated at the same table. Or walking around Miden, or in a bar at the port, watching the ships in the distance to charge our thoughts with intensity. None of us were prodigious talkers, but in such cases good manners go a long way. We were well-mannered people. My father, perhaps, would not have appreciated the wine in Miden, but how could you blame him. I could have asked him to stuff a few bottles to bring with him in his suitcase, even if that required another permit from the Import Commission. They would have tolerated a few bottles. The idea of tasting a decent wine again almost convinced me to invite my parents, but we would have eventually run out of alcohol, and it wouldn't be easy to speak among well-mannered people about my life in Miden. I couldn't even manage by email. So what kind of interesting things are you doing? my mother would ask. She always liked to add some nice words before a question: so, well, hey . . . It was her subtle way of showing she could be informal.

What interesting things was I doing in Miden?

I'm evaluating whether a lit candle inserted in the anus is evidence of rape, I should have told her.

That was another practice my boyfriend had spared me, but only because I suffer from a rather rare allergy to wax. I may have gotten over it, though. I never checked again.

# Him

My girlfriend started showing clear signs of paranoia. She was convinced that everyone was keeping her under observation. It seemed like a narcissistic delirium, because if anyone was under observation, well, it was me.

"At the most they watch you with disgust," she said. "I get compassionate looks."

I don't know whether she had just discovered the meaning of the word, whether she had never needed it in her private life up till then, or whether she had expressly looked it up in the dictionary, but suddenly "compassionate" had become a filler word for her.

"Stop looking at me with that compassionate expression," she would say when I brought her coffee in bed, when we played cards, or when I happened to caress her hair or thigh.

"I wasn't even looking at you," I told her once.

"Exactly. Just what I meant."

Experience should have taught me that there's no logic to these types of remarks, they're merely a basic expression of irritability, touchiness. If you keep your cool, you might wind up getting laid; otherwise it's better to pretend nothing happened. Experience, more generally, should have taught me a bunch of other things, but I never found empiricism convincing.

"You meant that I *was* looking at you with a compassionate expression, otherwise you wouldn't have asked me to stop," I retorted.

"Is that how you two got off, you and the girl? You corrected her and she got wet?"

# Her

My boyfriend asked me if I was jealous of the girl. He was neck-deep in shit and still worried about me being jealous.

"I broke it off with her before meeting you," he said.

"Yeah, you wish," I responded.

My boyfriend said I had become cruel. He started telling me a lot of unpleasant things. That I'd become cruel. That I'd become paranoid. That I'd become jealous. I think it was rather true, but the jealousy was the most disturbing because it was much worse than that: it was a complex form of envy. If I were older, I might have envied the girl's youth, which would have been sad but tolerable. Still, only a few years separated us. When I was in my own country, everyone told me that I seemed young for my age. It was true, I hadn't changed much over the years, but I shied away from such observations, and I blushed with the coquettishness of a little girl. I looked at my bare legs in those ankle boots, the skin of my thighs still tight. I soon realized it wasn't meant as a compliment. They weren't saying that I looked younger, but that I didn't seem fulfilled enough for my age. In the end, the Crash had voided any chronological subtlety. We aged and regressed; we could have been wrinkled babies or adults as smooth as silk.

After the girl came to see me, I couldn't get rid of her presence in the house. She was beautiful. Violently skinny. I thought that my boyfriend had never enjoyed such beauty while hugging me. It just wasn't possible with my body. I envied the girl and envied what he must have felt while possessing her. I wondered how many times that body came back to him in his dreams. I thought of his anguish when they separated. You get used to loss at the end of a love, but losing beauty must be dreadful. It had never happened to me. I tried to see it through my boyfriend's eyes. I imagined his days at the Academy in front of that body, and I felt a pain I hadn't known. I hated that pain. But I envied it with all my being.

# Him

I got a letter from the girl's father. Back then, she had often spoken to me about him. She'd been raised with the myth of her father. In her wallet she kept photos of him as a young man: a vertical strip of snapshots in black and white, wearing sunglasses in all four photos, with an affable smile and a leather jacket I'd seen the girl wearing. It was important to her that I admire his beauty. I don't know what kind of feelings she wanted to stir in me when she showed me those photos. I always had to be careful not to reveal my embarrassment, because it was clearly something she didn't know how to deal with.

My weakness pushed her away. If I had a fever, if I strained a tendon, she would look at me with a vicious distance. Any weakness whatsoever made her angry—even a headache, a cold with too many tissues involved. So I looked at the photos without betraying any unease. But I never understood why she was showing them to me. Did she want to offer me proof of her genetic pedigree? She never spoke to me about her mother, who could have been dead. She wasn't dead.

*I was one of the founders of Miden,* her father wrote. *I believed in that Dream. I want to keep believing in its justice. I know that you are also about to become a father. If one day you happen to receive a file regarding your daughter's sexual relations, I assure you it won't be pleasant. I'm not a violent man, in all my life I've never come to blows, but my first instinct was to hit you. I can't say that instinct has been assuaged. Perhaps I wouldn't even be able to hit you. You might even get the better of me. It's not important, that's not what made me drop it. Miden exists because we are not beasts dominated by instinct. I don't want to write you this letter as a father. As a father, I only feel hatred for you. I hope I never have to meet you.*

*I don't know what your life was like before you came here. Miden has been a haven for many, for others an escape, but for those like myself, who created it, Miden is an act of faith. It means believing in humanity. You must have taken an oath, sworn allegiance to the Miden Dream yourself. I don't*

*know what you felt at that moment, beyond the
ephemeral pleasure of a ritual. For my part, every
time someone pledges allegiance to that Dream, I
feel that my struggle has had meaning. For those
who come to Miden today it's hard to imagine that
there was really a struggle, perhaps because no one
had ever taken up arms, devastated a land, defeated another people. We never sacrificed human
lives, shed blood, erected monuments to our martyrs. We didn't have any martyrs. We don't want
martyrs. We want to be happy. That's our Dream.
That's what you swore to. Martyrs have sad faces—
proud gazes, but sad. They look to the future, and
yet they are dead. We are alive.*

In the corridor of the Academy there were portraits made by
students of the Miden Dream founders. Each was in a different
style, though the styles tended to converge in a single cartoon-
ish vision. Indeed, the faces betrayed no sense of martyrdom.
I never stopped to think about whether they looked happy,
but I have to admit that those faces transmitted a sense of
vital serenity. In part—I believe—this was due to the contrast
between those portraits and the work of my students, which
I'd grown accustomed to, where all vitality had been warded
off as if it were the plague. I asked myself if the portraits were
commissioned according to precise directives, some sort of

Midenite socialist realism, as if at the time of its foundation they'd made an effort to lay down some theoretical guidelines that would reinforce certain values, even though those values were limited to the dogma of happiness. Or maybe the portraits aspired to sacred art, and the mere fact of asking myself such questions betrayed all my bad faith. "I don't know what you felt at that moment," the father wrote. I tried to think back to the oath. What did I swear allegiance to? I had wagered on my future. That's it. And for a while it went well for me.

# Her

One night I felt bad. I had severe shivers, nausea. "I'm about to lose the baby," I said to my boyfriend in a flat tone. I don't know how seriously he took me, but he rushed me to the clinic. I had a fever, not much more. I wasn't losing the baby.

I wondered what would have happened if I had. Whether the community's attention would have shifted to this even more tragic event, like a nail pushing in another nail amid the general emotional apprehension. I decided that I would have instead added a perfect tessera to the tearful mosaic under construction.

In Miden there are no longer any diminutives or pet names (they remain only in nursery rhymes). They were eliminated from the language to keep women from being harangued in an untoward or debasing way. So they couldn't use the equivalent of "poor girl" for my situation, which was comforting. I'd often heard "poor girl" in my country. It was almost always a woman saying it to another woman. My mother was always going on about some "poor girl," referring to cousins, nieces, and daughters of acquaintances. There were various reasons why a girl would be saddled with that term: a failed exam ("poor girl, she studied so hard"), an abrupt weight gain ("poor girl, I didn't want to say anything to her"), getting ripped off in a shop ("poor girl, and she thought she was getting a bargain").

My mother called me poor girl countless times. It seemed like she was expressly waiting for a possible disappointment to console me in the soft embrace of "poor girl." One afternoon, when I had put some order to the things I was leaving behind in the house where I grew up, looking through old diaries and letters saved in drawers, she said to me, "Poor girl, you suffered a lot in your adolescence." My suffering never had anything to do with her. Obviously it never crossed her mind that reading her daughter's private writings could be considered disrespectful. When I pointed it out, her compassion became more full-bodied: "I'm sorry that you still need all these secrets." It was proof that I had things to be ashamed of, proof that, deep down, I was still a poor girl, even after crossing the threshold of maturity.

But there was an even more irritating use of that word. One of my friends, who sincerely aspired to have a "normal love affair" and yet tended to become a secret lover, always referred to the "official" girlfriends of the men she went to bed with as "poor girl." She especially liked to have these men recount to her the absurd excuses, alibis, and subterfuges by which they managed to carve out time with her. After which she would be there to dispense indulgences. "Can you imagine?" she said to me. "The poor girl is in the hospital getting a lump cut out and he's taking advantage of it to fuck me."

I was happy that I wouldn't be a poor girl for the inhabitants of Miden. And not even poor, for that matter, because that was another word banned from the language. Technically, there were no poor people in Miden, in the sense of indigent, because everyone had a standard of living consonant with their needs. And there were no poor in the sense of unhappy, because the society couldn't conceive of them. The only meaning allowed was "poor" in the sense of "lacking" (cholesterol, sodium, sugar, gluten, contradictions). So all the compassionate looks I kept getting had nothing to do with my emotional misery. I wasn't unhappy, I was merely a woman put to a test. Despite the trepidation, they were all convinced that I would come out brilliantly. In any case, my baby was healthy and safe in my belly. How could I yield to dejection?

# Him

*I'll vote against your expulsion,* the girl's father wrote me. I tried to imagine how much those words must have cost him, not so much with regard to me—the man he hated—but when it came to his wife and the girl. Neither of them agreed with his choice, so he wrote me: *They don't understand. Through Mediation they'll come to understand, even though they won't approve.* He was eager to let me know that he hadn't overlooked anything.

The Mediators were part of one of the most important Commissions in Miden and were subjected to constant monitoring and psychological stress tests in which they had to demonstrate their objectivity even in the most controversial situations—and what was often meant by controversy was just life. The Mediators were guarantors of the established order, even as they gave the impression that there wasn't any established order. They had a maieutic approach, trying to draw out the most obscure reasons for an estrangement or a squabble between two individuals. They tried to draw out from the black vortex of conscience the tranquil star of common sense. They intervened in family relations, in relationships between couples, in quarrels among friends, in cultural misunderstandings. But there were limits beyond which they wouldn't push. My case, for example, could not be examined by the Mediators; it was explicitly a matter of "violence" and "abuse." The vortex of my conscience was so black that it swallowed any glint of common sense. Fishing down there would risk soiling even the net, to use an ugly metaphor. It wasn't my metaphor, but one used by the director of the Commission one of the last times I spoke to her. "Let's not blur boundaries," she said, making reference—I think—to our previous friendship. The director had also had some sporadic contacts with my girlfriend. I don't think they really hit it off—not from any sense of antipathy, but more from genuine indifference. And yet, their meetings must have further blurred the levels of their relationship. In Miden everyone was very wary about "blurring levels of relationship," mixing the personal with the professional. They must have imagined their own existence like a building.

If my country had gone to the whores (and, alas, not just for a stroll), it's because there was so much blurring of levels that the building collapsed in a heap of rubble. Things were only done out of friendship, as payback, because of fear, threats, or out of spite. Wasn't that the reason I left for Miden?

# Her

I'd gotten into the habit of walking along the shore. I told myself that any kind of habit would be better than chaos, even though talking about chaos in Miden sounded like an oxymoron. I liked that word, it was very fashionable in my country. In the past few years there had been a relentless increase of oxymorons in our lives, in our emotional relations, in the newspaper headlines—a sort of epidemic. But chaos in Miden remained an oxymoron. So maybe I didn't need any habitual routine, just to do what I normally did: nothing. Above all, I would have had to accept that little dose of chaos as a blessing, because few received it as a gift.

As I walked placidly along the shore, I saw the girl running in the distance. Not running toward a radiant future or into the arms of a lover—as I would have imagined—but jogging. She surprised me. I hadn't imagined her staying in shape that

way, I thought she was more punk than that. She was no longer
the fragile, gloomy creature who had dropped into my living
room, but a healthy girl who jogged in a matching outfit. She
had an enviable ass. And in fact, I envied it. All my life I never
did sports, or rather, I'd stopped when I was a little girl. But I
admire people who do, even though it's hard for me to admit,
especially since it would be so easy to imitate them. I admire
people who have the candid self-satisfaction of doing something that's good for them.

Sports aren't exactly obligatory in Miden, but they are
strongly encouraged. The public parks are full of sports equip-
ment. The gyms are almost free of charge, and kids in their
last year of high school get their license to become personal
trainers. It's a way for the young to care for the adults. There's
almost one pool per inhabitant, and as soon as you get out
of the city, there are little natural lakes. And obviously, there
is the sea, even if it's always freezing. Those who don't get a
personal training license can get one as a lifeguard and accompany people who are incapable, like myself, of swimming
with a wet suit. It's almost impossible to deliberately ignore
all these stimuli. Even an invitation to play Ping-Pong makes
me uneasy, and so does the national sport of Miden, which
is a sort of badminton with two small balls. It was born as a
parody. It's an ironic sport. You play with irony. The basic goal
is to get confused, make a mess, and bust a gut with laughter.
Another effect is that of getting very upset. So almost all the

women of Miden have fantastic legs, well-tapered calves, and visible adductors. The kind of legs that look perfect with heels in a panty hose commercial. But high heels, apart from clogs, are not worn much. They wanted to encourage Miden's local craftsmanship, so they started producing low, very minimalist sandals, with a single strap to hold them on the feet. Usually they're made of leather, but there are also vegan versions. And then there are clogs. Just as minimalist, with that one thin leather strap. It's all local, kilometer zero—Miden cows, Miden wood—in part because imported goods make the inhabitants feel destabilized by the unknown. And yet, in that unknown, in the world outside of Miden, those shoes have become a cult object. Taking into account the exchange rate, they are ridiculously expensive. Many of my friends were happy that I moved to Miden, because I could buy and send them shoes without the extra charge. It was a clandestine operation, which I can't deny elicited a quiver of excitement in me. Then there were the handmade raw wool sweaters in Miden colors: small red or orange rectangles—like the houses—against a light gray background. When I went to the Academy parties, all my boyfriend's female students had those boatneck sweaters. With nothing underneath, they showed off the fine clavicles that I believe are a fundamental element of youthful eroticism.

I made all these considerations as my gaze followed the running girl. I wondered why I didn't wear clogs anymore, and long skirts and little necklaces, and all those hippie baubles that would have at least served to create a little noise and distraction as I walked silently in Miden. Then maybe people would look at me with annoyance and not compassion. Even in that moment, for example, if I'd had my baubles on, I could have called the girl's attention, but she was focused on her own rhythm. If there was anything she had kept from our last encounter, it was her distance from anyone else.

# Him

*People tend to sublimate unpleasant events in their
own lives, inserting them into a broader design.
As if our mistakes will always teach us something.
Often they convince themselves that it was all
somehow "useful." To me that's rhetoric for the
weak-spirited. I don't know you, and I can't judge
whether you've learned any lesson. But I'd like to
tell you one thing: do not make any effort to find
meaning in what you did. Make peace with your
mistakes. Live with your remorse. Don't try to
transform it into something else.*

It was clear that this man was looking for my admiration. Perhaps he didn't know that I had already been forced to show his daughter that I admired him, he didn't know that I had looked at her photos of him with a humiliating feeling of competition, he didn't know that those pictures had sometimes undermined my ability to get a hard-on. In the name of the Miden Dream, he was ready to vote against my expulsion without offering his forgiveness. I wondered what I would have done in his place. What kind of letter I would have written. And yet, I would have loved to wallow a little in my weakness of spirit, if I were indeed that sort of man. But I didn't even know how to respond to a basic question I'd asked myself: Would I have wanted the girl to look at me the way she looked at her father, or the way she had once looked at me?

# Her

I started to appreciate the narcotic power of music. I didn't want to hear stories, and the TV didn't give me anything but. And forget about films. I couldn't care in the least if someone escaped alive from a chase, if the kid who ran away from home would reconcile with his family, or if the uptight single girl would fall for her best friend from childhood. I wasn't interested in what others were doing. Surely they had something to say, but I wasn't interested in finding out what. Faces, events, stories. Everything tired me. I didn't even want to know about the news in my country. I didn't want to understand anything. I started spending many hours listening to music, something I'd never done in my life. Maybe it was my boyfriend's fault, the meticulous care with which he tried to structure my musical education: listening in chronological order, little riddles about the bass line. But there, too, I was trying to draw conclusions.

It was nobody's fault. Or maybe it *was* someone's fault, but who cares. I wasn't even able to say what I liked to listen to, it was enough to have the sound fill the house, take space away from the facts of the day, from the extenuating circumstances, from the girl's bony body, her ass in the jogging outfit, from my thoughts full of resentment. I even started to sing. Poorly, without understanding the words. I emitted only sounds. I hoped the baby would hear them, hoped he might learn to live outside of History.

# Him

One good thing about teaching in an art academy is that you can count on the students' flashes of inspiration.

The Commission had tried to keep quiet about my case so as to not compromise my lessons, but it didn't take long for rumors to spread in a community like Miden. In any event, the principle of due process held, so I was still considered an excellent teacher and a respectable citizen of Miden. (It couldn't have been otherwise, because there were no non-respectable citizens. Once you lost your respectability, you lost your citizenship as well.) But various parents protested to the dean of the Academy. Mothers and fathers equally respectable, genuinely convinced of "innocence until proof otherwise," nevertheless felt obliged to raise doubts "given the particular circumstances." It perked me up considerably when I heard about these doubts.

Shouldn't the teaching of philosophy also dispense moral precepts? they asked themselves. Was the Academy sure I was still the right person for such a task? Wasn't it risky? They wouldn't have objected, for example, if it had been my colleague, the professor of artistic anatomy, but with philosophy—you have to admit—it's a different matter . . .

Ah, what a joy! What pride! I would have liked to call my father and let him know that teaching philosophy was a time bomb. That his son was a walking disaster, merely a miserable incompetent who abandoned his country in its moment of need.

I wasn't present at the meeting with the dean of the Academy. I was only told what they'd talked about, so I never had the chance to reassure the poor nervous parents that there was nothing to fear; even if I were a serial killer or a perverted necrophile, my philosophy lessons had about the same impact on their children as a recommendation not to swim right after eating.

Despite the parents' fears, those smug, careless kids, happy to embrace danger in the flower of their youth, showed up to class one day wearing white T-shirts on which was written WE'RE ALL PERPETRATORS. I don't know if they all left the house that way or if they got together in the bathroom to change, but half my class were wearing that T-shirt, even the girls. Their audacity bordered on folly, considering that the word printed on their tempting breasts was "perpetrator" in the masculine form, an obscene identification, unprecedented and beyond my remotest imagination. They were together with me. They were perpetrating together with me, against the Academy, against their families, against the girl who that day seemed dumbstruck in her isolation. What I wouldn't have given to see her! Her cruel and wounded eyes. She drove me crazy when she put up all her defenses. For a time we went crazy together. Then we would have fun looking at everything we'd demolished. She would smile and mockingly sweep the defenses scattered on the floor. Then she would bend over to pick one up: "Here, this one's a gift." But that day I wasn't with her. I was against her, alongside a string of students with whom I'd never shared anything, apart from telling them to wait a couple of hours before going for a swim.

# Her

I suddenly started suffering from insomnia. My doctors assured me that my baby was sleeping well, but I couldn't fall asleep. I tried to concentrate on music. Then on his heartbeat. My boyfriend tried to make up bedtime stories; I told him to save them for our son. I hated stories. I hated his voice, too, but I let him read me poems. I didn't understand the meaning of the poems, so I found myself easily distracted.

I thought back to when I wrote poetry myself, and to a trip I took when I was twenty to see a guy I met on a train. He introduced himself as "the poet." We didn't want to tell each other our names. "But if the police stop us, we'll have to tell them," I pointed out one morning. What kind of worries did I have in my head, even then, at twenty, facing the poet who would write verse on my arm? It was all new for me, my first time traveling outside the country. I knew I had no hope with the poet. He would go on his way sooner or later, and I would keep worrying about the police. We stole everything we could. For no reason. And half the things we stole were abandoned along the way. One night when I couldn't get to sleep, the poet told me, "Count one sheep, then forget it. Then you can count it again."

And now I was doing just that, even though it probably wasn't what the poet had intended. In my insomnia I counted the girl who entered the house. Then I forgot her. And then she entered again.

# Him

Then came other T-shirts. Those were white too, the same make, same cut, without stitches, which I came to learn was one characteristic of a high-end T-shirt. But the writing changed: WE ARE ALL SUBJECTS. You had to admit, they were beautiful. It wasn't by chance: in an art academy, the students are very aware of style. And I wasn't the only one to notice, because in the space of a little time the T-shirts started circulating outside the Academy. By that point the writing no longer had anything to do with me. WE ARE ALL TREES, WE ARE ALL ONE, WE ARE ALL OBLIQUE, and other random words. My favorite was WE ARE ALL CHAIRS.

I believe they were sold outside of Miden as well. I can't be sure, but I think the students made a little money selling T-shirts and even bags with those phrases on them. The letters simulated a typewriter's typeface. Not so original an idea, but minimalism always seems to be profitable. In any case, for a week (dubbed by the dean as the "white week" because of the color of the T-shirts) the Academy was the theater for this vibrant clash of slogans. My pride got a considerable boost. My colleagues looked at me with something between indignation and incredulity. I read in each gaze an inflexible sense of envy. But why should we wish each other ill, if we could all be chairs?

A rumor started that the girl didn't want to leave her house anymore. But it wasn't true. I wonder whose idea it was to spread such nonsense, considering that in Miden it's practically impossible not to run into people on the street. Even my girlfriend had seen her jogging.

The dean didn't know how to stop the titanic clash of slogans. Her only worry, repeated like a mantra with powers of absolution, was "We must protect the students." I would have liked to advise her to make us a T-shirt. Then the white week faded out. There were only a handful of hard-core students who continued to wear the shirts. One of them tweaked it by tattering the collar, another liked to wear it over a button-up shirt. It was a clothing item with versatile charm. At the Academy, my issue was never openly addressed; the girls knew how to protect themselves on their own. I happened to eavesdrop on a few conversations in the halls, nothing more elaborate than a normal chat between classes. Even among the rival T-shirt wearers there were no big ideological dramas, and they exchanged the last drags of their anise cigarettes before going back in for the lesson. Slowly I realized that the real crux of the issue—unfortunately—had nothing to do with me. No one was taking my side, no one hated me. I wasn't the point of contention. If anyone had inspired the white week, it was the girl, watching from far away, from her sidereal distance, as I once used to sing. It was a harsh blow to my pride.

# Her

I've always loved shopping in Miden. It is one of those activities that makes you feel you are contributing to the well-being of society and not just your personal well-being. On every product is a label that explains the origin, process, amount of water consumed, and income distribution in the production chain of those who have come into contact with it. The label generally tries to have its own ironic narrative style, just engaging enough to make you a more conscious consumer. Among the jobs proposed to me, once I gave birth, was that of writing labels for preserves and detergents. I would have worked together with an illustrator. That wasn't what I'd imagined for my life, but I was comfortable with self-pity. Many of my friends who stayed home had spent their best years crying all over themselves and then regretted all their weeping. It's true that they're called the best years only when you regret having wasted them, so maybe there are no best years.

When I went to the market to buy tea and some strangely shaped pumpkins that grow only in the Miden greenhouses, I noticed more than one person with the same shopping bag. It was a white canvas bag with words printed in a typewriter font. A young woman beside me at the vegetable table, stroking the synthetic sheen of two perfectly spherical tomatoes, saw me and immediately turned the bag. But I had already gotten the chance to read the writing. I think it was one of my boyfriend's students, whom I'd met at an Academy party. But I always mixed the female students up, their pale complexions, blond hair, handmade sweaters, skinny legs. The girl left the two red spheres on the table and began to walk away, holding her bag against her hip. I bought the two tomatoes and followed her, tapping her on the shoulder. "Here, keep them," I said. She looked at me with embarrassment.

"Did you go to bed with the professor too?" I asked her with a certain brutality. She took the tomatoes and shook her head.

"What does that bag mean?"

"I use it to shop."

"What does that writing mean?"

"I don't want to get into it."

"You walk around with a proclamation on your bag and you don't want to get into it?"

The compassionate looks to which I'd grown accustomed became more anxious. Faces afflicted with worry popped up among the aisles of the market.

The woman shrugged her shoulders as if she were a little girl. I imitated her.

"That's it?" I asked.

She gave me a gracious smile, an easy admission that she didn't know what to say, then shrugged her shoulders again with the same grace, making fun of herself. We stood there shrugging our shoulders at each other for a bit. She smiled, I smiled. But her smile became nervous as we continued to shrug at each other in a paroxysm that wasn't easy to stop. My smile, however, was serene. The bystanders' anxiety continued to grow. The lady who sold felt slippers meant to protect parquet floors hazarded a similarly mocking gesture, putting one slipper on each hand and moving them around like two puppets. One hand aped the other. A few long faces betrayed amused grins. I had no problem continuing to shrug and smile serenely. The young woman must have begun to feel stupid, and I couldn't blame her; we looked silly, but not in the cute way she would have hoped. The tomatoes I'd given her created another hassle. I started staring at them, wondering what she intended to do. Stuff them in the bag that was causing all those problems, or hold them in her hand like an inept juggler, with a puppeteer behind her waving two slippers? She stopped. She emitted a forced snicker that sounded vaguely swinish.

"You know, like, the bag is cool, isn't it?" she asked me.

"No," I said.

The woman stopped her slipper show. We both relaxed our shoulders.

# Him

My girlfriend decided that night had to become our hell. During the day she didn't speak to me. At night she stayed awake, and I felt her gaze on me like that of a vulture on a carcass. When I opened my eyes and asked what the matter was, all she did was stare. She got up. Put on loud music. Then came back to me. At that point I was awake. "Do you want to talk?" I asked. And she responded by singing. It was her new thing, singing. "Tomorrow I have an early class," I told her. But she kept singing. "Or maybe nooo . . ." she warbled. Someone at the market had told her that they intended to fire me. Or rather, to suspend me until the witnesses gave their evaluation. My girlfriend had a very intense relationship with the market. It always seemed as if she were going on an expedition to see the oracle. She no longer had any interest in what was going on in the world. All she needed was the market. Whenever I watched a news bulletin, she grumbled with scorn. "How many migrants drowned today?" she asked, laughing. I didn't find anything funny about it. But neither did she. "Can we talk?" I begged her at night when she kept me awake. Yet every morning, despite everything, I continued to bring her coffee.

"Didn't they advise you to get therapy?" she once asked me. "Why do you want to talk to me?"

She showed me all the therapy flyers they'd given her.

"What do you say? Does this suit me?" she said, posing with the flyer in her cleavage.

"Or better pale pink? Speaking of which, do you remember the dress that—"

She didn't finish the question.

"What?" I said.

"I don't know what I wanted to say."

"Can we talk?"

She put down the flyers she had in her hand. She looked like she was hurt, an animal that didn't know where to flee. I watched her soft body as it kept our child inside with all those words. Then she burst into tears.

"I want the life I had back!" she shouted.

"Me too," I said.

Tears streamed down her face, as they had during our first nights together. It was cruel to admit that I liked the desperate docility of her weeping. I missed it.

"Not that one," she said. "The life before."

After so long, we found ourselves united again, in the longing for something neither of us knew how to explain.

# Her

The visitors no longer came. I wasn't the one who chased them away. I had the feeling not so much of being avoided as of being left in peace. I've noticed that the only time people tend to leave others in peace is when the others have never been further from peace. So they left me, and that's it. I still got the same looks outside the house, but no one ventured to set foot inside. Too bad, because I would have finally known what music to put on for the visit. Once you begin to regret something, it's easy to get carried away. It all becomes a matter of focus.

I tried to remember afternoons spent with my boyfriend coming up with a list of names for the baby. We, like everyone else, tried to think of names that went well in every language, in every country of the world, imagining our son's future as we had once dreamt of our own. All that was left of that vision were fragments, poorly assembled like phrases in a book whose plot doesn't hold together. I tried to zero in on a detail, but my gaze settled on an intermediate distance. It wasn't a lack of memory; I would have been able to rewrite that list of names, remember our comments, the attempts to invent new words, the game of mental associations, me making fun of my boyfriend for his inability to roll his *r*'s, and him coming up with names full of *r*'s. This was still in focus. His hands on my thighs were also in focus. Me kissing his neck. Also in focus was our laughter over the names of our grandfathers and uncles. And the affectionate, playful way of sifting out similar elements from our past, as if we'd left behind a common story. The story of his childhood mixed with mine. And our youth. Who knows what we were trying to show, abandoning our country and then talking about grandfathers. The same people kept popping up: peasants, cobblers, laborers, or trade unionists. We needed so little to love each other.

# Him

The first questionnaire to arrive was my tutor's. According to protocol, the Commission had to examine the questionnaires and then send them to me for the sake of transparency—not just informative transparency, but emotional as well. They were supposed to prepare me for the verdict on many levels, raise my awareness according to their holistic principles. It was important that the witnesses provide an account that "heeded the nuances," that took into consideration "possible cultural conflicts" and expressed their opinions without separating them from any "sentimental sincerity." The tutor was a nice guy, my age, always available, sharp, able to forestall a wish before you even had the chance to formulate it. When I got to Miden, he had greeted me with open arms, which is the code of welcome. You open your arms, and then you embrace the new citizen, trying not to overwhelm the other with your own body. He was the one who processed my candidacy at that time. He was struck by my musical tastes and how I drew "hope." Actually it wasn't me who drew it, it was my brother. He'd read my application and found it cold. So he did a sort of revision that made it more touching—or ass-kissing, depending on the point of view—and then drew "hope" because I wouldn't have known what to draw. But I did draw the tree near my signature. The tutor never noticed the difference in lines, not to mention creativity. He didn't even comment on the little tree (it was more a toothpick with two skewed little arms), but hope—an abstract fresco in which my brother claimed you could make out the shape of a newborn humanoid—had "sincerely struck" him. And so did my whole candidacy application, for that matter, considering I'd been accepted. There was one phrase in particular from my application that the tutor repeated to me for months, as if it had changed his life: "There are works of art that we've loved in their reproductions. But the reproductions don't teach us anything, they don't prepare us for the moment when we're given the chance to see the works in person." I would never have written any such thing—that was my brother's doing. But the gist of it was that I didn't know what to expect from Miden; you understand things only when they're happening.

For his part, my brother felt like a prophet when—much later—he found out that I was going to be a father. I'd obviously forgotten about his drawing. But he, unlike my-self, was attuned to allusions and prophecies. His was an emotional, mystical memory. When my case broke out in Miden, I happened to think back to that drawing. To my little deception. I'd been accepted, in part, on the basis of a lie. My musical tastes, though, were authentic. And in that area I'm much more sensitive and creative than my brother, which in a certain sense might render me an even more treacherous imposter.

It was the tutor who showed me my house for the first time, raising a toast with me to the Miden Dream, showing me around the Academy. I'd already noticed the girl, and she'd noticed me. An unequivocal gaze passed between us in the hallway. I'd fantasized about that gaze for days before winding up in bed with her. They weren't just sexual fantasies, although I have to admit they were mostly sexual. I saw her in another way. I had just gotten to Miden. Notwithstanding the fact that the tutor was my guardian angel, my confidant, my devoted friend for weeks, I felt lonely. My neighbors brought me welcome sweets, loaves of colored marzipan, they introduced me to their babies, they made me gifts of hand-knit scarves and asked me a host of questions about my country. Young mothers and young fathers, together with their children, all caught up in listening to my funny stories. I made them even funnier than was needed. They were so well-disposed to me that they would have let me wear them out with some preposterous dream made up on the spot. They studied me, amused, and I let them, because that was precisely the aim of their gentle interrogation: to sketch out a laughable caricature of my country. I let myself play the game and didn't find anything strange in it. It was a feeling I'd already experienced in my travels as a boy during study-abroad stints; when you go to a new place, it's part of the rules of engagement to feign ignorance. You wind up drinking with someone you wouldn't normally hang out with, tell your story as if it were a parade of absurd anecdotes. It's a way of getting to know people; you can't be too subtle about it. Or so I told myself.

I felt lonely. And I hated marzipan. Not to mention hand-made scarves. I thought the age for wearing them had long gone. And then I remembered one of my ex-girlfriends who always gave me handmade scarves as gifts. She had a devastating dedication; to judge by the heap of scarves she'd given me, she must have spent her entire life knitting. At one point she even started selling them on the street. She sat down amidst the buskers and unrolled a sheet on the asphalt. I never passed by, because I was ashamed to see her cast into the street among the stockinged legs of ladies doing their shopping downtown. Then one day I caught her at the flea market, rifling through the used scarves in search of merchandise. The ways in which an affair can end are incredible.

Anyway, those first few nights in Miden, as I was moving through the house, I had only the girl's gaze to latch onto. She didn't watch me as if I were a strange creature, she just looked at me. I felt her near me. We'd noticed each other in the hallway while the tutor was taking me by the hand, as a friend, a brother, a companion, showing me a future full of trust.

# Questionnaire No. 1
## The Tutor

*You were the professor's tutor. What kind of relationship did you establish with him?*

I became his friend.

*Your final tutorship report was extremely positive. Do you feel you made any errors in your evaluation?*

I'm still thinking about it. I wonder if our friendship may have compromised my clarity of judgment. I love my work and believe I've matured over time and developed a complex sensitivity for the human soul. I wouldn't want this to seem like a presumptuous statement in the eyes of the Commission, I'm not a presumptuous man, but I've come to trust my intuition. It's part of my profession, and I try my best to serve the Miden Dream. Anyone who thinks that sensitivity is an innate gift is mistaken. It must be cultivated, like everything. It's a matter of craftsmanship, requiring care and the will to improve. The more it's honed, the more it becomes spontaneous. Even enthusiasm requires application. It might seem paradoxical, but that's exactly how it works. My sensitivity led me to believe that the professor could become not only an exemplary citizen of Miden but also a dear friend. Now I'm tormented by the fear that I may have blurred our relationship.

*Do you remember your first meeting with the professor?*

The day the professor first arrived in Miden was my birthday. It was an unusually clear day, and the sky was striped with pink. The rocks that lined the desolate road from the airport looked like giant quartzes, as he himself commented while admiring the view from the window of my car. Excuse me for delving into such detail, but I was happy that the professor could enjoy such rare beauty in his discovery of Miden. He certainly wasn't the first foreigner entrusted to me, but his candidacy had sincerely struck me. Perhaps it was naïve on my part to welcome his arrival as a gift for my birthday. But I'm wary of those who don't know how to appreciate the signs, and I believe that only the envious can accuse others of naïveté.

*In the course of your relationship, did the professor ever speak to you about the young woman?*

Yes. When the professor told me about the girl, shortly after his arrival in Miden, I was disturbed by the casualness of his words, but I wasn't surprised by the revelation. The first time I accompanied him to the Academy, I immediately noticed a look pass between them. At that moment, though, perhaps out of willful blindness, I chose to underestimate the significance of that gaze. He talked to me about the young woman several weeks later. Then he stopped. When I asked him about her, he was evasive. I asked him if they'd had an affair, and he said no. Only later did I find out that it wasn't true. Perhaps I should have reported his lie back then, in my final tutorship report. I didn't do so because I attributed it to a weakness on his part. I saw in him a man enamored who looks to protect the object of his love. It was neither a matter of censorship nor of clemency, but of trust. I thought I was acting for the best, because I was sure that the professor would soon realize the inappropriate nature of his relationship. And in fact, time proved me right. The professor ended the affair with the student. At that point he himself told me the truth. He needed consolation from a friend.

*If yes, then how did you judge the relationship between the professor and the young woman?*

At the time, I didn't have the proper clarity to judge. We sometimes talked about women, yet there was something

particularly obscene about the way the professor talked
about his student. At times I felt uncomfortable with his
abrasiveness. He teased me, made fun of my prudishness
and my straight-arrow nature. It was part of our friendship.
When he drank more than he should have, he let himself
go and confided things I imagined had been distorted by
the alcohol. He had an urge to possess that had nothing to
do with love. Still, I felt I had to justify him, even though I
couldn't empathize with him. I thought that being uprooted
from his country had led to a sort of sublimation, a transi-
tional phase that accompanied the violent shocks of adjust-
ment: the desire to possess another body because a land had
been lost.

*Do you know the professor's partner?*
Yes.

*If yes, how do you judge the relationship between the professor
and his partner?*
I was the one who facilitated his partner's acceptance to
Miden, even though her candidacy was not among the best
received. I don't judge applications on the basis of merit, but
on the quality of the dreams. We don't need engineers to
build our roads, we need happy people to travel them. The
professor, though, needed a partner. I realized that his life
here was incomplete; love at a distance intensifies desire, but

distance deforms it as well, it wears out the spirit. I wanted
to believe I was acting for the best, even though I was a bit
hasty. I even expressed my doubts to the professor. We were
in a bar by the sea. He listened to me, continuing to stare
at the horizon, as if on the other side of that line there was
a land he hadn't been able to forget. I was born in Miden, I
saw the Dream grow. I don't understand that kind of nostalgia. At times I regret not being able to experience it. I realized that what the professor felt for his partner, what they
shared together, was something I had never felt in my entire
life. This realization, instead of estranging me, brought me
closer to him. We wound up drinking an entire flask of
absinthe. In the sweetness of the sugar melting in the glass, I
felt part of his story. I, too, awaited the arrival of his partner, and sometime later we all celebrated the news that they
were expecting a child. I felt overwhelmed by that intimate
familial joy. The Miden Dream would have the privilege of
three new citizens united by happiness. I was proud of my
role in bringing these two together. So much so that perhaps, yes, I indulged the sin of pride.

*How did you react to the student's accusations of violence?*

When I received the file from the Commission, my first
reaction was disdain. I thought the girl was taking revenge
against the professor. I didn't know her personally, but I
know how blinding one's resentment can be at a young age.

I even ventured another theory, that the girl was trying to hurt her parents with those confessions, that it was an irresponsible act of rebellion. Only now do I understand how wrong I was.

I remember meeting the professor outside the Academy. He invited me to a bar, but I refused, not wanting alcohol to erode any responsibility for our words. We sat on a park bench and talked while the students passed in front of us. The professor looked at them without any particular emotion. He didn't seem tormented, only bothered. Even my own concern bothered him. "So what do you want?" he asked me brusquely at one point, as if I'd become his enemy.

"I'm on your side," I said.

"I'm on no side," he replied.

*How do you judge your conversations with the professor following the student's accusation of violence?*

The professor didn't deny anything that was written in the file. His position remains the same. I admired his honesty, and still do. Nevertheless, I lost respect for him. It mustn't have seemed like a grave loss to him, considering that he, I now understand, never felt any respect for me, nor for the student, nor for his partner, nor for the Miden Dream, nor for TRAUMA no. 215. But I'll always have some fond memories of him.

# Her

I came to Miden thanks to the tutor's intercession. He had already examined my boyfriend's candidacy, and he took care of my application. In our long-distance communications it was hard for me to distinguish between the zeal of a bureaucrat carrying out a protocol and the sincere interest of a friend looking to reunite two lovers. Thinking back on it now, I don't believe there was a substantial difference. I can say that the tutor acted as a friend trying to optimize the development of a love story. There's no need to dwell on the disconnect he must have felt later. Human beings are always inherently torn, by temperament, nature, or existential quirks. And anyway, I felt more torn than he did. Why had I prepared my candidacy for Miden? I spent days questioning myself about the real reason. My answers changed and came apart, pieces were added to them. How many practical considerations had already stained my supposed choice of love? We were no longer inured to romanticism. For years they'd spoken of us as a lost generation. When investigating the events that had condemned us to the Crash, no one had asked us if we were in love. We didn't even ask ourselves. Unhappiness was measured on another scale. Indeed, unhappiness had vanished from our conversations. There were only inconveniences, frustration, stagnation. Something had been irremediably broken, they said. We didn't even have the courage to use certain words. Without any children to take care of, we took care of ourselves with the angry compassion of those who had never chosen anything. Even our distress seemed desolate. Deserted, we looked back on that age of anxiety with nostalgia. Each one of us cradled a random memory and tinkered with it for days and days. And somewhere within that mass of memories was the image of all that had been lost. It could have been the end of high school, the chorus of demonstrators just before the bludgeons, an unruly lock of hair in the breeze, a trip to gather mushrooms, a train ride, soft-pack cigarettes.

I thought of a memory that was much more recent and livable: our tent flapping in the wind on the Miden beach, the arctic cold outside, and my boyfriend holding me tight. I decided I missed him, and wrote him a bunch of emails. I embellished my memories. The love inside our shelter—and my boyfriend had a job. The sex was magnificent, the thrill of his body, and I was able to get welfare for a year. "Dress in layers, like an onion" he wrote to me, among other suggestions, as I was about to leave for Miden. I liked the fact that he took care of me from a distance, that he imagined my body under so many layers, keeping out the cold. For my arrival at the airport in Miden I tried to look sexy, even though I was dressed like an onion, but I didn't know what to pack for the rest of the time. (How long would I stay? How many onion layers should I pack in the roller suitcase?) In the end I packed only what I thought was cute. I picked other clothes by following the sole principle of cuteness. "Keep covered," my mother kept saying. "Dress in layers," my boyfriend said. "Do you need money?" my father asked. Surrounded by all that affection, I prepared my giant roller suitcase. I was happy.

I soon discovered that dressing in layers was one of Miden's regulations. When I landed at the airport, I received a pamphlet in which a group of people were photographed first nude, then in sporty undergarments, and ultimately looking like polar bears. That pamphlet captured the Miden spirit for me—the ironic and carefree depiction of nude and imperfect bodies (though actually they were all in shape) subsequently fused in a uniform woolen awkwardness. In the same pamphlet, an elf with an otoscope unrolled a poster illustrating "bad" objects. The objects were anthropomorphized, their malevolence expressed in spiteful mean-faces. "Our ears," the elf said in a bubble, "are made to hear the pitter-patter of a fawn in the woods." In the iconography of annoying sounds depicted in the poster, the roller suitcase was rendered as a huge piece of luggage, all arrogant and full of itself, its two wheels endowed with spikes. My boyfriend had forgotten to warn me. I was the only one with a roller suitcase. As the wheels crossed the halls of the airport, I received only a few delicately embarrassed looks, but once I was outside, when the wheels rattled as they came into contact with the asphalt, I saw a woman plug her child's ears and two girls wince with sudden pain. My boyfriend was happy to see me, but we had no way of hiding the roller suitcase, considering that it came up to my elbow. I burst out laughing at the absurdity of the situation, and he kissed me instinctively on the mouth. Only later did I realize that he kissed me to keep from attracting any more attention with the noise.

# Him

The tutor suffered like a dog in writing his responses to the questionnaire. I felt bad for him. I imagined him racking his brain, searching for the words that would offend neither me nor the Commission. And then other words—words of impotence—to give substance to his moral dilemma. I believe that was his real torment. He had nothing exceptional with which to torment himself, but I let him anguish, because it was clear that he got an almost sexual pleasure out of it. (I had no idea what else could give him the same type of thrill. I'd never seen him excited, apart from when he was anguishing.) He didn't look for signs of remorse in me. Not right away, at least. Instead he sought an entry into what must have seemed to him an impossible abyss. It wasn't my intention to prevent him from gaining access, but it's hard to open wide the door to an abyss if we don't feel it. He wanted me to show him the stigmata of my corruption so he could stick his finger inside, horrified, and feel the thrill. But I continued to talk to him stubbornly of love. He shook his head. He couldn't stand it and plunged back into his anguish. So eventually I let him in. Gave him whatever he wanted. A violent relationship? Unspeakable violence! Abuse, degradation, shame. Here, take all the horror you can handle. He needed his dilemma: to be the friend of a despicable man. I did it for him. I was his abject friend. And yet, I kept talking about love. And that was when he shuffled the cards on the table and started haranguing me about remorse. But c'mon, that's unfair. That wasn't the deal. I couldn't be the one who drew the character arc of his conscience. He introduced himself as an innocent young man, then an accomplice, then a redeemer. "I'm confused," he said to me. Never get involved in others' confusion. Especially if you have no desire to take them to bed.

# Her

The first responses to the questionnaire started to arrive. I liked having something to read together with my boyfriend. When we met, we would get together and lie down in the tent, flipping through the same book. The camping lantern silhouetted our bodies. What usually happened is that we'd chuck the book aside and start fucking. Reading the tutor's questionnaire was the least erotic experience in the world, so it was hard to get my libido going. I knew the tutor was never crazy about me, but I never thought he was secretly in love with my boyfriend. It would have been an almost touching infatuation but for his wallowing in resentment during the waning phase of that sentimental thrall. Not that I cared what he thought, but for the sake of decency, if they ask you to analyze *my* relationship with *my* boyfriend, you could at least avoid all that stuff about your own complex role as procurer. It seemed not only out of place, but even off-topic. He just didn't get the question. I think I had a mildly hysterical reaction to his questionnaire because I burst into laughter without being able to stop. Usually laughter is contagious, but my boyfriend seemed content to sit there unmoved, apparently studying the neurotic source of my giddiness. It wasn't a good feeling, but I continued to laugh. Then I stopped. I thought about my own responses to the questionnaire. I stayed on topic. I carried out my task. Why hadn't it occurred to me to make an impression when the possibility was offered? The tutor had even described the sky's pink highlights. Not to mention the "giant quartzes," even though it was my boyfriend who first came up with that image. He must have liked it a lot, considering that he recycled it on one of our first nights together in Miden. "Don't they seem like giant quartzes?" he asked as he led me out of the tent, holding my hand. He asked me that question as if I were a little girl. In those days he often spoke to me as if I were a little girl. And I nodded like a little girl. Who knows if he remembers? Later, I didn't ask. By that time I was busy chasing down more insidious concerns. And if I had asked for my questionnaire back in order to embellish the answers? Would I have seemed ridiculous? It wasn't my style to scatter pink highlights and quartz dust through my writing, but I could certainly have talked about myself. My life before Miden. My life beyond the sea. A castaway. Where did I come from? There was more beauty in that question than in the Miden Dream.

I felt sick just thinking about it. My boyfriend hugged me; he thought I was offended by the tutor's words. For a moment I mulled over whether to enjoy his hug and forget the rest. But I no longer knew what I should forget. My recalcitrant mind came back to my questionnaire. Had the Committee already read it? If my candidacy wasn't among the top, then my questionnaire wasn't even remotely satisfactory.

# Questionnaire No. 2
## The Swimming Instructor

*What are your relations with the professor?*

I'm his friend, I believe.

*How did you meet him?*

We go to the same pool.

*Do you remember your first encounter with the professor?*

Yes. I remember him staring at my legs! Not that he's ever stopped! ☺

*Have you ever noticed sexist attitudes in the professor's behavior?*

Apart from looking at my legs? It's a thorny question. The professor comes from a culture very different from ours, and I believe that certain mind-sets are hard to defeat. If you're used to focusing on parts of a woman's body, then it's not easy to take it in as a whole. Though it's not really my place to say, I wonder if it might not have been more useful to pair him with a cultural mediator—rather than a tutor—during his first days in Miden. Moreover, the professor is certainly not a troglodyte (with all due respect to troglodytes), but an intellectual, so it was not always easy to discuss sexism with him. He always found a way to turn the tables and make it seem like even his sexism was natural . . .

*Do you know the professor's partner?*

Yes. I've met her a few times.

*If yes, then how do you judge the relationship between the professor and his partner?*

Back then I didn't see them together much, so this is just my impression. To me it seemed as if the professor's partner lived a little in his shadow. She doesn't seem to have integrated much into Miden life. In fact, she's always on her own. I know that they're both registered in Organic Pesticides, but my best friend, who is also in Organic Pesticides, told me that his partner hardly ever participates in the discussions and initiatives. According to my friend, she signed up only because the professor did. I also know she was exempted from the tutorship period because the professor himself was her tutor. In my opinion, that wasn't a good idea. The way I see it, it would have been better to assimilate into Miden society independently. The bond between a couple is surely important, but community bonds are more important. Especially if you come from a culture so different from ours, a culture where the role of the woman is unfortunately still subordinate to that of the man. I've read certain things about their country, many interesting articles, and if I can allow myself . . . they have a long way to go! I think it was a mistake to overlook those factors.

In any case, on the rare occasions when I saw them together, his partner was rather taciturn. In the beginning I thought it was shyness, but now I think it's a symptom of indifference, or a passive-aggressive attitude. I, for example, have trouble speaking when I don't sleep well. I invert syllables, can't remember words, so I might seem more laconic than usual if I haven't slept enough. Now people understand that if I'm quiet, it's nothing against them. But we shouldn't look for the source of the problem in the language, as much as in the fact that I didn't sleep well. Thanks to a sleep therapist, I've discovered things I never knew—for example, that female insomnia is very different from male insomnia. After all, melatonin is a hormone, isn't it? They asked me lots of questions: Do your eyes change with the light? Do you prefer sweet or savory tastes? Do you have more strength in your arms or in your legs? So my point is that you have to delve into the causes, not the symptoms. Obviously, that works only if someone wants to know themselves and improve. For me, improving oneself is a moral and civic duty. I always teach that to my students. It's the first thing I say, and if I see them looking a little skeptical, I'll spend the whole lesson explaining it to them without even letting them get into the pool. They can complain all they want, but one day they'll be grateful. And not just them, their families too, their friends, their life partners, their cats, the whole society. Isn't that the Miden Dream? Whereas his partner was always quiet and warmed up only when she drank, and then all she would do was complain about the Miden wine. One time I courteously suggested, "Why don't you deal with it in the Organic Pesticides group?" She looked at me as if I'd just uttered some sort of gobbledygook. Exactly the kind of look I don't like! I'm a pragmatic woman. Complaining doesn't help anything; in the long run it only leads to an accumulation of negative energy. Speaking of which, I'd like to also point out that the partner is always wearing gloomy colors. I have a degree in chromotherapy, so I know what I'm talking about. I've often seen her wrapped in her gray coat, which she wears almost as if it were armor. Gray is no-man's-land. It's the color of indifference, the color of fog, the archetype of ashes. It indicates the need to defend oneself, to seek shelter in anonymity. Even when she got pregnant, she kept wearing that coat. She suffocated the baby under that gray blanket. You don't need to be an expert in chromotherapy to understand the symbolic violence inherent in this coercion. So, through the professor, I gave her an orange poncho with a floral pattern. That way she could put it on over her coat and activate a reverse energetic process without necessarily triggering a substitution that at this point could prove damaging to the baby. Orange cleanses the chakras and stimulates creativity and the immune system (very important in pregnancy!). It also expels toxins and instills enthusiasm and optimism.

To be honest, I've never seen her wearing my poncho.

# Him

I started wondering whether I'd be a good father. I was surprised that the questionnaire neglected this question. Wasn't that a fundamental point in considering the prospect of my raising a family in Miden? There was a great deal of enthusiasm at the news of the pregnancy—smiles, hugs, bad drinks, and then silence. A tangle of congratulations turned into a tacit suspension of judgment, as if, after the resounding applause at the end of a concert, the spectators lifted the collars of their coats on the way home, disturbed by their own enthusiasm. That suspension couldn't last forever. In a sense, I was in it too, with my own collar raised. I never shared my girlfriend's paranoid temperament, but she was right about one thing: the pregnancy had been transformed into a sickness of uncertain outcome. She was a sickly woman beside a controversial man. In other times I would have been cheered by that ambiguous vision of myself. I would have seen it as proof of a complex, ephemeral personality. But I was no longer so young. I no longer had that ambition. I just wanted to be a good father. And I wanted to know how others saw me in a parental role. Reading the questionnaires was a wonderful perversion, like finding an email about you open on the computer. Denigration feeds narcissism too; what's important is that they talk about you. And yet, no one expressed an opinion about my impending fatherhood. In my search for answers, I had even begun reading horoscopes, but astrologers are incapable of writing in concrete terms. They write sophisticated cryptographs to be deciphered, an irritating hermeneutical exercise garnished with a bland irony. I was certain that the failed students in my classes would find excellent jobs writing fun and useless horoscopes, even though the concept of failure was unthinkable in Miden.

# Her

"Let's get out of here," my boyfriend said to me in an upswell of courage—or cowardice. "We can still do anything we want."

"It seems you've already done enough."

He's always had an obsession with pioneers. But maybe he lacked the right spirit, a certain penchant for canned beans, a lone-wolf air about him. You don't go exploring the frontier to fuck girls. Pioneers stay on their own, around a campfire. At the most they take a stray kid on as their own. They fare forth across the desolate earth. Anyway, I would've had to find another dole. And splitting the vittles would have been less romantic than imagined.

# Questionnaire No. 3
## The Photography Teacher

*How would you describe your relationship with the professor?*

I'm one of his colleagues at the Academy. We don't have
a close relationship, but I respect him as a teacher and a
person. I chat with him readily, even though I've never seen
him outside the Academy. I don't know why we've never so-
cialized outside work. Maybe I didn't want him to think my
friendliness was a forced social ritual, something that would
make him feel like a trapped tourist covered in a garland of
flowers. I preferred to give it time.

*Could you list three of the professor's positive qualities and
three of his defects?*

I believe a person's qualities and defects tend to get confused. It's hard to separate them. A quality can turn out to

be a defect in certain circumstances, and vice versa. Allow me to make the only distinction of any value for me: there are people who are interested in others, and there are people who are indifferent. I'm not talking about altruism, I'm talking more about curiosity, or vision. A certain fervor of the heart; I can't say it any better than that. It's something very evident in my students, in their way of approaching a subject, in the intention behind it, in their willingness to get involved. The professor doesn't merely contemplate the world; he takes part in it. He has his prejudices, but he's a passionate man.

*Can you describe the first time you met him?*

It was at the Academy. He introduced himself, shook my hand, apologized for his pronunciation. He asked me to repeat my name. Then he repeated it too. He waited for me to correct him, but I had no objections. I remember he was well-dressed, wearing a dark green velour blazer. You don't often see a man wearing a blazer in Miden. I don't mean that the blazer made him seem out of place; in fact, it looked good on him, gave him a certain air of elegance. It looked so good on him that I was convinced his eyes were the same dark green. Actually they were brown.

Come to think of it, I find it very significant that the professor wore that blazer. He had just moved to Miden; those were his first days at the Academy. Someone else—in his place—would have tried to blend in, not stand out. I'd always tried to do that when I traveled the world as a freelance photographer, before I began teaching. It's pointless to try to conform through clothes; you have to study the ways of a place as you would the customs of a tribe. Miden is a tribe from my point of view, though I know many of you will be horrified by such a statement. Anyway, I don't mean that the professor was an eccentric type. Far from it. In reality we're talking about a rather sober blazer, but it's his distinctive trait. He was the only one who wore a blazer, and you understood, it seemed to me, that he was attached to it. That he had put it in his bag with a certain amount of affection, like a memory. In short, I got the impression of a man with some aesthetic integrity.

*Did the professor ever disrespect you?*

As I said, the professor is a man interested in others. He loves to discuss. For me this is a form of respect. Indifference is a lack of respect. He worries, for example, about not boring others in his company. I find that to be a worthy concern.

*Do you know the young woman?*

Yes. She was in my class.

*Did the professor ever speak of the young woman?*

Yes, but certainly not in romantic terms. We're not close enough to confide such things. If we talked about the girl, it was about her academic path. I had never noticed any favoritism on his part. Or rather, nothing that made me suspect extracurricular activity. But this consideration is somewhat problematic, since we should always engage with our students in a broader context. How could it be otherwise? Isn't that our task? The professor appreciated the young woman's intelligence, even though she didn't excel in his subject. Nor in mine, for that matter. Both of us, however, agreed on one point: as a student, she did as little as possible to get by. I'm the exact opposite, so the young woman aroused my admiration as well as my antipathy, but that's another discussion, and I'm working on myself to balance out my own relationship dynamics.

*Have you ever noticed any sexist attitudes on the part of the professor?*

I think it would be impossible for a sexist man to teach in classes composed almost entirely of women and maintain the professor's level of dedication. It might seem optimistic of me to see things this way, but I'm convinced. I don't deny that I've heard him make sexist jokes. And they weren't particularly funny—not because they outraged me, they were just outdated. I got the impression that politically incorrect

humor is still fashionable in his country. For that reason
his humor struck me as not so much out of place, but out
of time. I shouldn't be so indulgent, but those sorts of jokes
only stirred in me a kindly feeling, the same as I have for
people nostalgic for hard rock. I imagine it's more complicated to organize a revival evening of passé humor. Irony
just gets stale with age. If it stops making you laugh, it loses
its quality; it's not a whiskey that improves as it ages in the
barrel. That's why I believe the professor will shed certain
habits. He can't handle the sight of an audience bored by his
dated sense of humor. The velour blazer won't be enough to
protect him.

In my own travels I've also tried to win others over by
being brilliant, or using whatever I had. But this created a
cognitive dissonance, and it took me a while to realize it
could produce spiteful reactions. It was a form of vanity you
find in romantic explorers. Entrusting myself to that vanity, I've taken a lot of ugly photos. All that emerged was the
froth, a tropical light that was too intense, expressive faces
brimming over with life. It was blinding. That light didn't
exist, and neither did that life. It's easy to fall in love with
images that are so estranged from one's own reality that they
seem even more real. And yet, I was the one projecting that
estrangement, and the instant I recognized it, I thought I'd
grasped something. It was exhilarating. The beauty quickly
faded. The tropical light seemed noisy, the expressive faces

like comical masks. It wasn't easy admitting to myself that I understood nothing of a place.

The professor seems to be a man who latches onto certain habits of his bygone life. I find it very human to chase after youth, after what will never return. I believe he has idealized many of the things he believes he has lost for good.

# Him

I've never had a direct relationship with death. Two of my grandparents are still alive, the other two died before I was born. I've never lost any friends, relatives, or parents of friends. I've never been to a funeral. I've never had pets that could abandon me, apart from a goldfish that I insisted on throwing back into the water. I don't know if this is why I have a somewhat corrupted and limited idea of irreversibility.

I've often heard people say "we're at the point of no return." I considered it merely an expression. In fact, I do think there's the possibility of return. I couldn't imagine those points—like islands in the ocean, sunk into the water. You can always return, if that's what you want, but if you don't want to return, there's no need to hark back to Atlantis. Even when I left my country, I didn't think I'd reached a point of no return. I don't like that kind of ecstatic desperation. I find it criminal. That's how a murderer needs to think: "I couldn't do otherwise."

But ever since I started seeing the responses to the questionnaires, I felt increasingly nudged toward a malign point of no return, carried adrift by sheer momentum. I put up no resistance, a dead man floating, at the mercy of the waves, wind, and the words of others. I was surprised by my photography colleague's assessment. That whole paean about my ability to be interested in others, written by a woman in whom I had no interest. It's as if she'd captured something invisible to me. My bogus detachment, that couldn't-care-less attitude. The cheap arrogance. You despise what you desire when you can't have it, my mother always said. The truth is that I'd grown fond of Miden. I felt good here. I liked teaching. I liked the smell of the Academy. Organic turpentine and the hormones of young bodies. Watching my students overcome their shyness and change hairstyles. They came to see me after lessons with the vulnerable enthusiasm of someone who has just had an epiphany and can't wait to share it. They got worked up over fatal and fragile questions, as if the world's destiny were in their hands. And it was, in a certain sense.

I liked waking up in a house where nothing spoke of the past. And yet I used my own regrets to cover the fear. I came up with new ones every day. I wrapped them with care. I thought back to my country like a wistful old fart I would have once hated. The idea of leaving Miden terrified me.

# Her

Do we really know the person we love?

I would have liked to feel the weight of such a doubt, the shiver along my spine at the sudden revelation: discovering that you don't know the person beside you. But as I read the responses to the questionnaires, it didn't seem like I was unearthing anything new about my boyfriend, just like when I read the letter from the Commission. Instead I felt like I was being asked another question: Do we really love the person we know?

They were compiling an encyclopedia entry about my boyfriend, all working as a team, with open content. Even I had contributed my share.

I confess that I shivered for a second when the photography teacher used that beautiful expression: "aesthetic integrity." I saw my boyfriend's forest green blazer in a new light. Or rather, in an old light that had regained its splendor, through the eyes of another woman who appreciated his style, as had happened to me when I first met him. Miden was full of emaciated boys with fine blond hair, formless wool sweaters that covered their hands, quick elfin eyes. My boyfriend ironed his shirts, he never had holes in his gloves or socks. When he had a beard, it never had the rancid odor of food. There was nothing childish or unfinished about him. When I first met him, he was a man in every respect, a distinguished figure with aesthetic integrity. Without ever mentioning that possibility, he seemed like a father even before I got pregnant. He was so like a father that I played the little girl. We joked about my filthy skirts and hippie necklaces. On him there were always buttons to unbutton, belts to unfasten, blazers to take off. And during the lazy days of my vacation, stripping him was one of the few activities that kept me busy. Access to my body was less complex. All you needed was a gesture to undress me, or—more simply—it was enough to slip a hand under my skirt.

Did I, too, have aesthetic integrity? To judge from how I transformed myself after a few months, I'd say no. I'd have pathetic scenes in front of the mirror. I practiced a gaze charged with intensity, made faces with my mouth. I inspected myself for a long time, talked to myself without uttering any words. In films these intimate feminine moments in front of the mirror are always revelatory, the reflection disclosing occulted truths. There was a tenderness to my features that I didn't know how to judge. I was expecting to see signs of damage due to my insomnia and recent paranoia, but it seemed that everything was polished by an unsuspected inner peace. My skin was taut, luminous. The girl had absorbed beauty through her trauma. I was looking for mine—the deep gouge she must have dug into my features—but the baby I was carrying inside me tinged my flesh pink, smoothed my hair. I had a healthy, blooming glow. What kind of torment could a such a healthy woman possibly allow herself? Nothing more than a veil of sadness over her face.

# Him

While waiting for the verdict, I was kept away from the Academy. The dean called me in the morning and told me to stay home. She advised me to take a walk in the unusually sunny weather. "I'd like to go for a little stroll myself," she said with a phony caramelized voice.

"But . . . shouldn't I tell my students in person?" I asked.

"No."

The illusion evaporated all of a sudden. It was the first time I heard "no" pronounced so assertively, a no as intimidating and crystalline as the air of Miden.

"The students are going through a difficult moment," she added. "It's better for everyone to take a little break."

Naturally I'd already heard similar words in my life.

"Let's take a break," my first girlfriend told me when we weren't even twenty. Back then, time had a different quality to it, and taking a break meant the opposite, it meant letting things flow, pulling away from the stagnation to start living again. But now I wouldn't know how to fix that break, and it struck me in all its monumental weariness.

"I'm sorry," the dean added before hanging up.

"Me too, very sorry."

I walked out of the house without saying anything. I wasn't ready to speak to my girlfriend yet.

So what are you supposed to do? You wake up in the morning, you get prepared, you walk out of the house, pretend to go to work, and then?

You get to the point where you grow fond of your own imposture, like an arrogant chain-smoker staring at a spot in the distance for hours and crushing the butts under his shoe. Sitting on a bench in the park. Reading the newspaper front to back. Waiting for the sunset in a place where the light dims gradually. I couldn't picture myself doing it.

Around the time I would have been finishing my lesson, I got a phone call from a student. He invited me to his studio to show me something.

I had been to students' studios many times before. During my relationship with the girl I often went to hers in the middle of the night to fuck in her little room. The next day, when she returned to finish the project, she would get turned on imagining herself under the table or tied to a sawhorse as if crucified, and I would get turned on imagining her trying to work with the memory of herself moaning naked in the room. In her letter to the Commission she underscored the fact that my violence had even invaded her creative space and so was even more cunning and malicious. It was a manipulation that kept her from being free in her own space. It's true. That was the reason we liked fucking in there, so that every fantasy would be polluted, so that we wouldn't be able to feel free of each other.

One night I went there later than usual and found her curled up in her chair wearing only a large checkered shirt. On the chair there was a sign written in my language: YOUR WHORE SLEPT. HIT HER.

The clumsiness of that sentence was terribly endearing. I took off her shirt and kissed her all over. She was so happy when she woke up that she kept repeating, "Hit her! Hit her!"

She couldn't really pronounce it right.

But she carried on, singing jokingly, "Hit, hit."

"C'mon, stop it."

She wouldn't stop saying it, and I started to get irritated. She no longer seemed endearing, she was petulant. Selfish. I was disturbed by the mangled sound of my language, her mannered little-girl voice. I wanted her to keep quiet. I slapped her in the face. Backhanded, hard. I'd never done that, and she got scared. I got scared too. I apologized more than once. I hugged her as if she were about to burst out crying, but she stayed stiff in my arms without saying anything at all.

"Do you forgive me?" I asked.

"Yes," she replied.

Maybe it wasn't true. And maybe fellatio wasn't an unequivocal sign of her forgiveness. In that moment I wanted to think that it was, I needed to feel her close to me, and having my cock in her mouth seemed to me a form of closeness. It wasn't even pleasurable. I came quickly so that the ugly night could be over. It's the only episode that pains me to remember. And yet, she never mentioned it to the Commission.

The following day, in class, she still had the slap mark on her face. You couldn't see it well, a light red, but her translucent skin hid nothing. That morning I couldn't take my eyes off her. She sensed my unease, but there was no challenge in her gaze, as perhaps I would have wished, nor was there pity, as I had feared. Only distance.

I apologized again in the hallway outside of class. She cut me short. "Enough," she said. "I can't stand people who apologize."

A few days later I gave her a comic book in my language that I had ordered expressly from my country. I wrote her an inscription I hoped sounded funny: "To work on your pronunciation." I don't think she ever read it.

The other student's studio was identical to the girl's, but much tidier. It felt almost like a punishment to be brought there, recognizing everything and nothing. On the wooden table, just like the one that had loomed over the girl on all fours, there was a sculpture the student had just finished.

"I made it thinking of you two," he said.

"Us two?"

Then I understood that "you two" was the most beautiful gift I could have wished for. I knew the student and the girl were friends, but he had never spoken to me about her. It seemed that no one before that moment had ever recognized our union, but now we were the inspirational "you two." The sculpture was called *Solution to the Porcupine Dilemma*. I had talked about that dilemma in class: "On a cold winter's day, a group of porcupines huddled together to stay warm and keep from freezing. But soon they felt one another's quills and moved apart. When the need for warmth brought them closer together again, their quills again forced them apart. They were driven back and forth at the mercy of their discomforts until they found the distance from one another that provided both a maximum of warmth and a minimum of pain."

I remember that the students took notes and seemed interested in what the porcupines were going through, perhaps more for its fable-like quality than for its deeper meaning. It ended, "So as not to feel cold or pain, the porcupines kept a moderate distance, and for them that was the best position."

On the student's table there were two smooth porcupines, shorn of their quills, presumably made of modeling clay. They had a fragile but happy air, staring at the fire in front of them, an LED flame burning from a little bonfire made of quills.

"An interesting solution to the dilemma," I said to the student.

"It's a gift for you."

He packed the sculpture in a cardboard box. To keep from seeming embarrassed and clumsy, I thought about asking him a few technical questions about the process, but I didn't know what to ask. I felt so moved, I was speechless, paralyzed by gratitude.

"Hey, you didn't by chance kill a porcupine to get the quills, did you?" I asked.

He flashed an indulgent smile, and I felt even more like an idiot, my box in hand in that familiar and estranged room. I thanked him in the same tone I would have used to give condolences.

How did you manage to fall in love with someone like that? That's what I imagined the student saying to the girl, leaning against the wall, smoking casually, sensually. It seemed like a more than legitimate question.

# Her

The Midenites have a word in their language that they proudly claim reflects their spirit. It can be translated roughly as "welcoming," but in a warm, cozy sense that implies the intimate atmosphere of the hearth fire. It was a word that existed before the Miden language was reformed by the designated Commission, and even then it reflected the spirit of the place. You heard it in the national anthem, scattered among verses about forests, birds, fire. It was one of the first words children learned, and the concept was taught like a catechism. It was the way young people, in the throes of their first infatuations, described an evening that ended well. Obviously it wasn't an explicit reference to sex, but if a first date wound up being intense and pleasurable, the evening on the whole would be described as "welcoming." After the language reform and the advent of the Miden Dream, the word's meaning expanded.

They tried to make the cemeteries, landfills, and intensive care units "welcoming." Likewise, they even pushed sex to the limits of embarrassment, obliging everyone to characterize it as "welcoming," regardless of whether it was a fleeting affair or a lasting relationship.

In the questionnaire they asked me if I deemed sex with my partner "welcoming." More precisely, they asked if my partner and I had the capacity to have "welcoming" sex. It's not easy for me to evaluate the good faith of my responses. I tried to navigate through sincerity, utilitarianism, apprehension for the future of my child (which could be classified as a more generous form of utilitarianism), and resentment toward my boyfriend for putting me in that situation and toward Miden for having generated it. Moreover, I felt I needed to manipulate events so that my role graduated from extra to costar. In those days it was easier for me to imagine my life as a screenplay. I wasn't interested in epic scenes, but in the tidy resolution of the drama. It shouldn't have been such a bizarre idea, because in Miden they even had therapeutic sessions that entailed role-play. They pushed people going through particularly confused moments of their lives to recount their personal stories as if they were film plots. Then they created scenes with actors. This was nothing new; the Family Constellations therapy that had become so fashionable in my country followed a similar process. But in that approach the mechanism was one of estrangement, seeing oneself personified in another. In my case I didn't need that distance from myself to "understand." Rather, I needed some events to happen. Since the girl's arrival at my house that day, in order to make these events happen, I needed action to form a robust, compelling plot. But I could only make out my own efforts. I was a shoddy, quixotic director. I felt doubly defeated from both an ethical and aesthetic point of view. I had failed to counter Miden's visionary pragmatism, its captivating simplicity. I thought I was more complex, full of contradictions, but I didn't have a shred of proof that I really was. Wasn't the doggedness with which they had managed to transform sex into something "welcoming" perhaps much more controversial? A doggedness that was then occulted with stylistic flair, leaving nothing behind but the final result in all its clarity. Meanwhile, I tormented myself by constantly replaying all the camera angles and close-ups. To get where? To unwelcoming sex? Was that really the extent of all my efforts?

# Him

I tried to take my release from the Academy in a sportsmanlike manner. Quite literally, I dedicated myself to sports. In the morning I went running on the beach. I'd stopped swimming, with the excuse that the chlorine irritated my skin, but the truth was, I didn't want to meet anyone at the pool. In the afternoon I played imaginary games of basketball. There was a basketball hoop in the driveway.

I imagined my boy in the future, in the phase when boys adore their fathers. I could see him forced to bear the boredom of those afternoons in the driveway. But perhaps we'd have fun, my son and I, or daughter—in Miden they don't allow parents to know the sex of the baby before birth so as to avoid any prenatal psychological conditioning. I built a cradle out of wood and painted it yellow, and my girlfriend drew abstract figures on it with a marker. When it was finished, it looked more like a doghouse, but it was beautiful, and I'd made it with my own hands. I looked at it with pride. We deserved such happiness. I'd spent three afternoons building the cradle. My girlfriend would smile as she passed me the screws, hugging me from behind as I measured. She nodded when I suggested "Yellow?"

"Shouldn't we consult with the chromotherapist?" she joked.

She welcomed me again with her irony. She welcomed me, and that was it. I felt like a prodigal son for her, and she for me. So if there were fattened calves to kill, we were ready. Our hands all smudged with yellow paint, wearing our work-at-home wardrobe. We dressed like a cute couple tinkering around the house together: she in overalls with her hair up in a kerchief, me in those Indian drawstring pants that were actually hers. Normally, I never would have worn those clothes, but in the photos we took, I looked like the man I was supposed to be. We looked like two young parents expecting a child.

Now that I was spending more time at home, I realized that my girlfriend and I had turned our house into a fortress against Miden's sinister glare. We worked with contrasts to subdue the sense of luminous rarefaction, of air, of vastness. The space had become more cramped than was necessary, going against the basic rules of interior design. Many pieces of furniture were intentionally out of place, even out of function, as if they were huge insects that had suddenly succumbed to heart attacks. And we, too, looked like giant moths knocking against the obstacles because we lacked vision, so I tried to convince myself that our vision had already taken our knocking into account, that it was the food our bond needed. And our gaze was shortsighted, yet warm and centered: What did we care about infinite space when the convulsive sizzling of a lightbulb would have sufficed?

# Her

And so our second photography phase began.

The first was during our courtship, when I was getting to know my boyfriend. I'd traveled around with my grandfather's old Rolleiflex, trying to make an artistic reportage of my vacation, which then transformed itself into a series of postcards made by neophyte lovers. Miden is particularly photogenic. My future boyfriend and I tried not to clash with the landscape. We took shaky portrait shots inside the tent. The black-and-white photos did their work, as did our desire. Those photos were what convinced me to move to Miden. Or at least that's what I told myself. In the end, what you tell yourself winds up becoming the truth. Then my grandfather's old Rolleiflex was left abandoned beside the expired rolls of film I'd brought from my country. As soon as I moved to Miden, I wound up walking through the city, wanting to take photos.

I wondered what effect any deterioration of the film might have, but I didn't find out, because I inserted the roll into the camera incorrectly and didn't manage to get any photos. The rest of the rolls were left to expire a little longer. One day my boyfriend took them and threw them out. I didn't protest.

Then came the second photography phase. We jokingly came up with names for it. Our blue period. Pink. African Arctic. Our shit period. Our expecting period. We built a cradle and painted it yellow, a color I'd always hated. It seemed like a good beginning. We tried to take photos for our child. We wanted him to one day see his parents as they were preparing for adulthood, even though they were already adults.

I had my side project, a challenge all my own. My parents asked me for photos of my belly, as if it were possible to feel a heartbeat through the film grain. I scrupulously denied them that satisfaction, sending them photos of our blue, pink, shit, and expecting periods, in which I was posing with my boyfriend. Two parents so busy that the belly was a distraction. You could never see my belly in the photos. There was my face, my hair under the bandanna. Miden's crystalline air. The yellow cradle. The paper butterflies hanging in the room. My body from behind, wider, but without any declaration. My maternal ass in silhouette. Could they feel the baby's heartbeat all the same? My mother always sent me a bunch of hugs in response. She never hugged me, but always sent me hugs. I sent her photos, subtracting the belly. She sent hugs, subtracting contact. We were two women who had never touched each other in their lives. I hated her body, and now I saw it appropriating mine. Some years ago I'd begun to resemble her. And she sent hugs to her daughter's body, which had become an extension of her maternity.

"It's your fault I won't ever have children," I'd shouted at her so many times. She never got upset and always gave that singularly irrefutable response: "When you become a mother, you'll understand."

And what did I understand now that I was becoming a mother? That there are dark places, deep miseries and sedated ambition under that timeless truth.

So I accepted her hugs and took photos. At times I was surprised by the unexpected beauty of my smile. I'll be a better mother than she was, just because of that, I thought. I didn't remember my mother smiling, not even in a photo. But that was a lie. We had the same smile, and she smiled in every photo. You don't have to be happy to simper in front of a camera.

# Him

I dreamt that the girl was apologizing to me. But she said, "You have to apologize too." And I said, "No way." And she said, "Yes way." And it went on that way for a while. Just like that, I said no and she said yes. But it was clear that she was having fun and provoking me. In the end we wound up fucking. Maybe it's a little wrong to call it a dream, because it started in a half-sleep, guided by my thoughts, but sex with the girl must have happened in my sleep, because I had a wet dream. I don't know if my girlfriend realized. I don't rule it out, considering that her insomnia, once pathological, had now become almost ideological. I got the impression that she was controlling me as I slept. I got the impression that she was controlling me while awake. She said she didn't want to lose intimacy with me. It wasn't control; she was keeping me from becoming a stranger. One morning she said, "Can we talk a little?"

She had a melancholy expression. For once, she made coffee for me. She drinks it black and can't imagine anyone wanting sugar. I appreciated the fact that she served it to me in bed with a glass of water. Those little gestures were important to me. I was easily moved.

"I answered the questionnaire too," she told me.

"I know."

We'd never spoken about her responses. In those days it took nothing for things to slide into the realm of taboo. The Commission had not yet sent me her completed questionnaire, and according to the regulations, I wasn't allowed to read it before they sent it to me. But no one would know. It was just a question of conscience—or rather, of induced conscience—as was everything in Miden.

"I wrote that we'd had violent sex."

Just the expression made me smile. It sounded like a vague porn category when you don't know what to look for.

"You did well," I told her. "But what does that phrase mean?"

"You know very well."

"No, I don't. It seems like a pretty generic concept."

She became even more melancholy, and I felt like an asshole. I was treating her like a member of the Commission.

"My love," I said.

We hugged. I felt the soft embrace of her body. I'd surprised myself in calling her that and was enjoying my sincere amazement.

"I feel like I've betrayed you," she said, pulling away.

"In what way?"

"I wasn't on your side."

It had become so easy to lose our moments of sincerity. She said she wanted to talk, then spoke in clichés. I thought of my dream about the girl, our playful teasing. More clichés. Was that all I was capable of?

"You did what you had to do," I said, continuing the exchange of insipid platitudes. But with my tone of voice I at least tried to convey a little trust—in her as well as in me.

"Do you think we're in love?" she asked me like a scared teenager.

"Yes, I do."

"And that's enough for us?"

"Of course," I answered.

"Why did you trust the girl? If she ruins our life, I won't be able to forgive you."

"That's like asking me why I trust you."

"It's not the same thing."

"What's the difference?"

"We're building a future. You didn't have to build shit with her."

She took her cup of coffee and walked away. I hate having to chase people. What's more, it was one of the rare occasions when I could enjoy coffee in bed. I heard her weeping in the other room. I tried to pronounce those words again mentally—"my love"—but I just couldn't. They were still true, but they'd lost all their weight. Or maybe the opposite; they were just heavy.

When she spoke to me of the future in that doomed and threatening way, I lost my mind. The future had become a form of blackmail. I heard her crying and couldn't get up. I thought about her forgetfulness and couldn't get up. What did it take to put a spoonful of sugar in the coffee? I started hating the future with all my being.

# Her

I could start the story like this:

*It's a holiday. The wind blows a gentle rain against the glowing windows of the house. There's ice on the streets and the parade seems to slide amusedly along the asphalt toward the sea. The banners hanging outside the window create the effect of a colored wave. Children file out holding hands. They wear funny hats and vests with the Miden symbol, a cute little fish with bulging eyes. The woman is facing the window, peeling an orange with hands red from the cold. She never knew the story of the fish, and she tries to make one up. She hears the children sing "Oh my little fish, I caught you, but you were already in my heart!"*

*And what's in the woman's heart? Creatures from a bygone time, memories that reanimate her. She recalls the nutrias around the lake in her faraway country. When she was little, her grandfather would accompany her there with a bag full of crumbs. She knew all the nutrias by heart. "They're rats!" another girl shouted to her one day to scare her, but she didn't get scared, because she could call them all by their names. One morning, there were no more nutrias. The lake was covered with water lilies. "Grandpa, where did they go?"*

*The woman had long been afraid of the water. The dark lake had swallowed her nutrias. Death nestled under the quilt of water lilies. But today the woman is not afraid of the water, and she doesn't fear death. From her window she watches the children walk by, and in her heart are the memories of what she was, next to her heart the pulse of what will be.*

# Him

It was on the Miden celebration day that I started to seriously think of leaving. I'd already talked about it with my girlfriend, but it was more of a rant, a moment of rage when you want to break away and be a rebel. With each passing day, as I read the questionnaires, blunted by their words, I started to really wonder what I was doing in Miden.

It was just like years earlier, when I was thinking about leaving my country. Something snapped, as they say in certain situations. This seemed to be one of those situations. I could allow myself to reason in terms of ruptures too, to put up some resistance to the flow of time. I was more mature than before, perhaps less sensitive to the allure of change, but as much as we diligently try to transform our lives into a comfortable cage, there remains a margin of resistance. Being childish for the sheer pleasure of it; feeling offended if things don't go the way we want and then threatening to give it all up. The more we delude ourselves that we make choices, the more we need to prove it to others. I felt like a kid who packs his things and thinks about running away from home. The only difference is that I chose that home in the first place. All the more reason why there was nothing to stop me from turning around and retracing my steps. All I had to do was change perspective; it wasn't me who disappointed Miden, it was Miden that disappointed me. It would be Miden that would regret my going.

The girl had endured TRAUMA no. 215, and I was enduring my own trauma. With a delayed reaction—just like her. Almost everything that had attracted me to Miden was now showing its deceptive face. In the official survey results, I would still count as a happy man. A happy man fearful of losing the things on the survey checklist that proved his own status as such. So fearful that he confused the fear of loss for proof of happiness. Perhaps the deceptive face was my face, the confident sneer of a boy preparing to flee.

After much time I realized that I'd left my country simply as payback, even if I didn't know what the payback was for. The individual motives of each person who left were lost in the great exodus. One day someone will write the definitive novel about our listless migration. We'll read it at a distance, so estranged from who we were that we'll be able to recognize ourselves in every detail. My ex-girlfriend who had gone off with my friend would embody the erosion of the welfare state.

All her tears in those last months sublimated years of social security contributions she never had a chance to pay. My sudden sexual impotence, those desperate nightly ambushes in an effort to rise to the occasion, my frustration as I prepared the application for Miden: these were all the interchangeable effects of the financial crisis. I convinced myself that I could get an erection again in a prosperous country. But the fact remained that I didn't have money to afford an analyst or to go to a doctor or a prostitute. So no matter what I believed, no one could contradict me. Anyway, there was no longer any reason to contradict. Our misery merely fed off our company, and love just bored us. This is shit, we all nodded in agreement; the shit accumulated, we got high on pot, then we could say good night and go to bed. My impotence lasted only twelve weeks. Then one evening I went to my mother's place. She was in the company of a colleague and her daughter. "Can you give them a ride home?" she asked. I gave them a ride. My mother's colleague stepped out of the car and winked: "You kids want to go out and have a drink?" She held out a banknote, as if we were still wet behind the ears. Her daughter immediately pocketed the money. "We're in a reality show about shameless mothers," she joked. I liked her immediately. I moved the car ten meters to roll a joint. She started unfastening my pants and I had a hard-on.

# Her

I could start it like this and end it in another way.

I, too, hung the banner out of my window on the holiday, but I didn't leave the house. I watched the kids walk by and didn't even lean out, didn't even expose my hand to the wind to wave to them. Entrenched in the house, I spied on them. Later the students would walk by. Then all the others, to gather at the beach, light a bonfire, sit around it—legs crossed, wearing oilskin fisherman's jackets—for a final concert. A band I liked was playing. My boyfriend had turned me on to them. The drummer was a student of his, a cute guy I once tried to chat up in a café with one of those pointless comments that was supposed to elicit a smile, but I ended up doing most of the talking. The guy turned out to be as taciturn as he was cute, so it wasn't my most successful pickup, but I liked the music they played and would have gladly gone to hear them had I not been terrified by the idea of sitting with my legs crossed in front of the big stage set up for the Miden celebrations, seeing as how I couldn't manage to hold that position for more than half a minute. And that was only part of the problem.

I hadn't shown up at the Organic Pesticides Commission to help set up our little procession; I hadn't shown myself anywhere for days. I hadn't made a dessert or a quiche, or anything else to bring to the beach for the evening. I didn't go to the window to wave to the kids, I didn't count off the number of days on the calendar until the big Miden party. My boyfriend had gone out that morning. "Let me see what the situation is like," he said. He'd never really cared much for the Miden celebrations, but he always went to the concert. At one time he also played music, back in our country. He let me listen to a few tunes, nothing original, but a couple of the pieces were cool. Then he stopped playing altogether, and it led to an extended and indefinite period of mourning. When he talked to me about it, I nodded, but I didn't understand. He never put it in terms of simple frustration, instead he described it as existential friction, which gave him a certain aura. The friction was like a violent form of diffidence that for him was vital and for me just seemed like trivial self-pity. Anyway, every time I said "C'mon, play me something," his eyes glazed over with sadness, as if to rue the fact that I just couldn't understand him. And in fact, he was right, because I didn't understand him.

I knew he'd thought about starting a band with the girl. Before things went south. I had even encouraged him to get in touch with her again. But he was an enigma. With every mention of the girl, he fell silent, as if overwhelmed by intolerable memories. I don't know why I kept pushing the music stuff for so long. Maybe I liked the idea of seeing my boyfriend with an instrument in his hand. It aroused me. In a somewhat perverse way I was even aroused by the idea of having this band of kids around the house, after rehearsals, before rehearsals, during an idle moment in the evening. I would have felt like part of the group, vaping weed in the living room, cuddling with my boyfriend while two others made out and someone else showed up in leather pants. It seemed exciting, even if I felt stupid for thinking about it. But all of us would have been stupid, a little stoned, a little wired. I would have come up with some cryptic lyrics, someone else would improvise a melody. The morning after, we would have laughed, mangling those lyrics, our mouths still pasty. I missed those laughs, hearing people make fun of me with a familiarity that no longer seemed possible.

# Him

I went home before the procession got to the beach. The sea ebbed away a little before I did. My girlfriend didn't even go outside. I found her in front of the window, like a figure in a painting. Her belly created the silhouette of a strange animal sleeping on the wall. I took the cap with the pom-pom that they'd given me on the street and slipped it on her head. I didn't know how to tell her. So I looked at her with the hat on her head and took a photo.

"Souvenir snapshot?" I asked her.

In that period we were taking a bunch of photos to document her pregnancy, so it wasn't clear what I meant.

"Imagine that one day this picture will define our memory," I said, throwing a vaguely apocalyptic light on my inability to express myself.

"Are you leaving me?" she asked, taking the cap off her head.

Her tremendous optimism always struck me. Up to now I'd managed to sidestep it.

"No. Actually, the opposite."

She looked at me, as if trying to figure out what the opposite of leaving could be, aside from staying together.

"We could be the ones who return," I continued mistily. "Maybe one day they'll talk about us as a generation. The generation that returned."

That evening I prepared a dinner that I hoped would be better than it turned out. There were days when my girlfriend and I talked fervently about our favorite childhood dishes. That kind of nostalgia already prevailed before people started leaving our country, before I left for Miden, before she came to join me. When the Crash started to erode everyone's lives, pockets of resistance were created around that distant communitarian principle: "Do you remember those tellina clams fished from the sea?" "The taste of hazelnut gelato?"

In those days it seemed that if only we could have grandma's sauce again, as if it were the primordial broth that had spawned us, we could set things straight.

The munchies after drawn-out nights of smoking pot had been more than just a chemical reaction; it was the need to tap into a heritage. We listened to songs on the radio. We were amused by the extravagant shallowness, the deft rhymes to keep the lyrics going; we reveled in others' foolishness because it vindicated the squandering of our intellects. Jesters wound up on the radio—not us, we wouldn't even come close. We sang the worst refrains without caring—the words weren't directed at us, we weren't obliged to feel those emotions. We made heaps of spaghetti with tomato sauce, and even that became a nostalgic ritual because we'd already been young that way, we'd already lived through that time.

Then we became adults, we went to restaurants, began our clinical dissertations about food. We hated each other, envied each other, imagined that we knew how to drink better than our parents. We furnished cute homes, accumulated magazines that talked about us, wrote for magazines that talked about us, picked out the right music, produced it, dished out geometric steak tartare, planted dill and lemon thyme. We even grew the best weed and stopped smoking dirt. And then there we were again, back to being housemates because we couldn't afford the rent after the Crash, sunk into a second youth, this one imposed on us, where we knew how to distinguish between good wine and swill but didn't want anything more than the belated consolation of a heap of pasta with tomato sauce. It became evident that we had no choice but to leave, unless we planned to spend the rest of our lives getting wasted on cannabis and carbohydrates. As exiles, our social media profiles were filled with attempts to recover all the food that had nurtured us. We posted photos of food we knew, recipes that never came out the same as they did back home. There was always something wrong—which seemed funny—in the shape, the color, or the consistency.

That's how we talked about our faraway lives: "What did you cook today?"

Other forms of love, which were just as communicable, eluded us.

But now that I'd made a decision, that was the form love took: my girlfriend, my son, my country.

I seemed to have so many pasts behind me, I wouldn't have known where to put the girl.

There was no more room to welcome her. There was nothing I wanted to give her.

In my memory it continued to be the best sex I'd ever had. But the sad thing was that I'd never get it back—not even in my imagination.

# Her

"We could be the ones who return," my boyfriend said to me. It sounded like a horror film plot. But we would have been milder zombies; we hadn't seen horrors that made us mute, we hadn't known death, we weren't thirsty for blood, only for good wine.

Unpacking is an extremely annoying operation, and I've often left luggage untouched for entire months after a trip. I would justify my laziness with a sense of doom, as if it would actually be painful to stick my dirty laundry into the washing machine, slip my shoes into the empty spaces in the shoe rack, take my makeup out of the beauty case stained with lotion. I pretended I could detect an oppressive determinism in that pretense of new order. So I let the luggage clutter the corridor or threw it into the corner of my room, an intentional form of procrastination, although I knew it was my own sloth that inspired it. Still, I grumbled when anyone complained about the encumbrance, and I sighed so pathetically that it drowned out any desire to retort, if only with even more pathetic sighs.

Leave me alone, was what the sigh meant, exactly the same message that the luggage conveyed.

And yet, there is that first exciting moment of unpacking your bags, when you pull out the things you bought during the trip. Gifts, a bolder-than-usual dress, a novelty snack. If I imagined that moment, then the idea of going back made me happy, a happiness that was simple and light, one I hadn't felt in a while, like a successful surprise party. My friends and I would try on the clogs in front of the mirror, and I'd give the bars of dried fish to little cousins who would give a lick and then spit in disgust. I would show them my photos and we'd take even more: my father posing in raw wool mittens—*in Miden they all wear them, Dad*—my mother with her poster of a film I'd never heard of, chosen only for the turquoise background, her favorite color. I would try on the cap with the pom-pom. I like souvenirs. They don't have to show anything, they have their own stories, and that's enough. I could spend a whole afternoon, for example, choosing a nice hat to flatter my face. If I imagined my return in those terms, I would get the impression that my life was nothing more than the flow of similar afternoons. But the cap with the pom-pom would always remain beyond such worries, beyond the little theater of insecurity and approval. I loved its docility. All I had to do was put it on my head like a cup on a saucer.

# Him

The day after the Miden celebration, they put up posters on the street with a group photo of everyone on the beach, everyone harmoniously distributed along the shore, each wearing a silver-colored mask shaped like a circle that covered the entire face, with two holes for the eyes and a big smile for a mouth. They looked like stylized children's drawings. Some held hands, others held meditative poses. The photo accentuated the stylized effect: the contrasting tones, the flat sea behind them, the clean line of the horizon. WE ARE THE PEOPLE was written in the sky above the parade of silver masks, the letters simulating cirrus clouds colored to harmonize with the landscape. It was my academy that came up with the idea of the masks. For entire days the kids had cut out circles of silver cardboard, lots of bright, identical spheres meant to represent the inhabitants of Miden as what they were and wanted to be: the people. Social equality behind the round masks, happiness restored in everyone's smile. There was no traumatized girl in that photo, no answers to any questionnaires, no me. There were the people, *happy people.* My refusal to attend the celebrations and the group photo made me feel even more like an outcast, and that was the noble version. In the more honest version I felt like a peevish kid who, instead of donning a mask, holed up in his room to pout. The soccer club calls me back to play with them after they'd kicked me off for a bad foul, and I don't show up. What an idiot. I was offered a second chance and I refused it, even though it was just temporary. But that's how carnivalesque role reversals have always worked. So why not enjoy it. Even in history's most unjust and ruthless societies, hordes of miserable people and outsiders had been able to enjoy reversing the hierarchies for a day. So why couldn't I enjoy it too? This was what I taught at the Academy. It's always been an alluring concept for the students. Maybe it leads to a latent desire for revenge, or vanity, maybe it seems frivolous and profound at the same time. In any case, I reversed nothing. I didn't put on the smiley mask, I merely stole that cap with the pom-pom to give to my girlfriend as a token.

The idea of abandoning Miden before even hearing the verdict forced me toward a sense of alienation, a confinement in which I would cling to my girlfriend and our future child. I cultivated both comfort and resentment, as well as a nagging migraine. I was an adolescent and an adult man. I can't say that we felt like a happy family, maybe not even a family, but that's who we were, and that's how we wanted to be.

Whenever I saw the billboards scattered throughout the city, though, I longed for the Miden spirit. The first game with the soccer team. The carefree competition. You can only be ironic about things you're still a part of. The irony of the outlier is pathetic. In my country we all grew up as part of something. We all went to parties and had fun. We harvested grapes, picked oranges, took ramshackle trains, pogo-danced at concerts, took part in demonstrations, protested against the police clearing out squatters. We reveled in our weariness. The social gathering after stomping grapes, the political songs at sunset, the popular dances, waking up near the embers of a bonfire that still smelled of smoke, or on the lowered folding seats of a train—it was incredible that you could still smoke inside the local trains—and we were always so tired, weary, legs full of lactic acid, as if it were lymph running through a single organism. Then came the distance, the harsh words. My friends held grudges against the enthusiastic holdouts. We wrote sentences full of scorn for what we had once been. We shared them. They blinked on our telephone screens. It all seemed ridiculous. Shitty losers, my friends thought. "Shitty losers," they typed on their keyboards. We hated the generations before us and held the new ones in contempt. We wouldn't let anyone else feel as weary as we had in our best years. Addled and comatose, we injected ourselves with lethal apathy.

WE ARE THE PEOPLE, said the posters on the streets of Miden. I would have said it too. Just a few years earlier, I would have shouted it drunk on the national liqueur while holding the girl. I remember when I marched in the procession with her on the way to the beach. The semi-secret nature of our affair seemed like a craven precaution on that holiday. We even kissed in public. A chaste kiss on the lips. And then she went on to kiss half of Miden. She jumped up and down barefoot on the sand to give away her kisses; smacking her lips, she pushed away the hair that the wind had blown into her mouth and kissed the people. We were all the people, and she kissed all of us. Admittedly, she was high. We all were. Swathed by natural MDMA, homemade and organic. When I found myself back home in the morning—which was no longer morning, but a long day already dissolving into the afternoon, an infinite night that had ridden out the hours, years, cosmic cycles, entire youths—I was dead tired. The girl was with me. We were always tired then. We never slept. In class I had red eyes, and she had perfectly beautiful circles under hers, black diadems on a white face. The memory of that weariness makes me cry.

# Her

The disposal of heavy waste has never been a big problem in Miden. One, because there is little to dispose of; two, because the Disposal Commission, like everything else, is very efficient. But the category "heavy waste" includes things that in my country you would have thrown into the dumpster, or, more probably, next to the dumpster, as they were always full. I had developed a bird phobia because of those dumpsters. There were months when no one came to empty them. Going for a walk had become repugnant, as had drinking a beer outdoors in the sticky, fetid air. The newspapers warned of epidemics and an invasion of rats. We expected them, but the rats never came. There were only birds. Seagulls that grew bigger every day and cannibalized the carcasses of smaller birds, blackened feathers and innards dismembered among the pizza scraps. Layers of guano on the ground, like sleet that wouldn't melt.

In Miden, when you stare at the sea, the birds cut grooves through the horizon. They beg timidly for crumbs that fall under the tables. They chirp in the morning to announce the new day. But I continued to look at them with suspicion. Sooner or later they too would soar into a rapacious nosedive to pounce on the organic waste, on the cadavers, on our remains. I didn't trust their eyes.

We hadn't turned to the Heavy Waste Disposal Commission to get rid of my roller suitcase, because we had a plan in mind. It had been a long time since we'd gone for a ride in a car, so my boyfriend rented one. We loaded the roller suitcase into the trunk, easing it in like a coffin in a hearse. We drove toward the forest, the car windows open despite the chill. We heard our breath as we tried to open our lungs. The only time I'd ever been to the osteopath was when my back went out; he had me lie down and he started pressing on my diaphragm. It hurt like hell. I was blocked there, he said. All the pain—I thought at that moment—all my pain depends on this point in my stomach. I didn't think then that the pain would take other paths, that my stomach would contain another life. But back then I often thought about my diaphragm. If I had only paid more attention to its deaf complaints, maybe I could have unblocked my whole body, all my thoughts. I imagined my child manipulating my diaphragm from inside to give peace to his mother. What could it do with its little hands? From the window I breathed cold

air and thought of my child. Was he able to feel the Miden
breeze? Could he feel anything?

The forest welcomed us like a Gothic cathedral. The landscape
didn't change gradually, but went from tundra directly into a
monumental block of trees. We left the car at the entrance to
the forest, dragging the roller suitcase behind us. Our ears may
have been made to hear the pitter-patter of a fawn in the woods,
but the wheels of a roller suitcase were like the clattering steps
of a new kind of predator. And if the fawn were to flee, pitter-
pattering through the woods, our ferocious beast would follow.

I burst into laughter.

"I have to ask you something," I said.

"Go ahead."

"Do you remember when I moved to Miden? I was laughing
about all the noise the roller suitcase was making . . ."

"Yeah?"

"Don't you remember?"

"I remember I was happy to see you."

"You were happy, but you kissed me on the mouth to keep
me from laughing."

"I kissed you because I was happy."

"You didn't kiss me because you were happy."

"I kissed you because I was dying to kiss you."

"No."

I fell silent, pausing to savor the vastness of the silence, and
from the bowels of the forest came the screams.

# Him

We went into the forest to bury my girlfriend's roller suitcase, and then we started to hear the shrieking. Desperate human shrieking. My girlfriend was frozen with fear. I hugged her tight and felt her body flinch in my arms. We were still on the edge of the forest; it would have been easy to turn around and run back to the car. But we didn't. I'd never heard anyone scream so fiendishly. And it was more than one person. The screams started multiplying, rising beyond the treetops into the sky. Then suddenly they stopped. Were they all dead? Another single scream tore through the silence. It subsided. And then another. And still another. A sequence composed of screams.

# Her

My boyfriend understood before I did.

And yet, I'd seen those flyers everywhere. At the market they would always hand me a couple of them. I had filled the house with flyers in that never-ending season of advice.

# Him

We abandoned the roller suitcase and headed toward the screams. In a clearing in the middle of the forest there were ten people gathered in a circle. In the center of the circle was a woman miming the movements of an orchestra director. Their choreography was interrupted by our arrival.

"We didn't mean to disturb anyone," my girlfriend said.

"We're here to welcome you," the woman said.

The circle opened out to make space for us. Behind us the trees marked off the natural curtain of that open-air theater. You could smell the forest and the sour odor of dry mouths lacking saliva, dehydrated. I recognized the mother of one of my students in the group. She was purple in the face, and I didn't know whether she was annoyed or embarrassed, or perhaps it was just her skin's reaction to all those screams. She glanced at my flashlight and waited in silence for a response.

"We're here to be free," the woman in the middle of the circle said with a benevolent smile. "If you don't feel free, then leave the circle." She was the group therapist. My student's mother gestured assent, breathing in deeply to give more depth to her conviction. No one left the circle. Then the therapist lifted her hands again.

"Scream!"

We started screaming. They seemed like expertly guided screams, responding perfectly to the cue. Some threw themselves to the ground in a convulsive lepidopteran dance, some dropped to their knees, some pulled their hair, some punched hard at the air in front of them. I felt stiff, embalmed in my position. I took a few hesitant steps toward the center, just to do something. I'm someone who screams with his hands in his pockets. My screams were ridiculous compared with those of the others; I was a novice. Beside me my girlfriend screamed as loud as she could. I barely recognized her. Majestic and beautiful, a priestess pregnant with sensuality. There was no desperation in her voice, no fear, no hysterics. She wasn't crazy, didn't betray rage, hate, or discomfort. She was perfect, so calm. She screamed with an unreal peace. In total control, ascetic and present. I looked at her with admiration. She was the best of the group. I yearned to possess her like never before.

# Her

I heard the voice of my child take possession of my body. I screamed with my entire being, but it was the being inside me that was screaming.

A birth before birth.

A painless wail.

The baby's gentle voice filled the whole forest.

# Him

She was the most beautiful woman at the party.

That's what I thought when I returned with my girlfriend to retrieve the abandoned roller suitcase. She was spent after the screams, plunged into a dense silence, her muted thoughts already far away.

"It did us good to scream," I said.

I spotted some gray strands in her hair. I hadn't noticed there were so many, or maybe they'd recently increased. For the first time, I thought about us growing old together, and it was almost a reassuring thought. We no longer needed to force each other to grow.

"We didn't scream together," she said.

I pulled a shovel out of the suitcase and sunk it into the soft earth. My girlfriend wandered around in the forest, then came up to me and took the shovel out of my hands. She wielded it in

the air and started digging, pummeling the ground violently. I
saw her rise up and come down with jerky movements, breathing heavily. It didn't seem like the most suitable exercise for a
pregnant woman, but I had the feeling that trying to intervene
would have led to a spade in the face. So I let her be. At that
moment I wasn't even clear on why we had brought the roller
suitcase into the woods to bury it. The previous day we had
spoken of leaving Miden as lightly burdened as possible, and
that suitcase was pure ballast. But we could have just left it in
the living room together with the rest of the stuff rather than
sinking it into Miden's bowels. The upturned earth emanated
an odor that reminded me of moments when I gathered moss
with my father for the manger scene we would set up under the
Christmas tree. I liked arranging everything before we put Jesus
in on Christmas morning, sculpting the landscape: the patches
of green among the pebbles, the water from the well made with
aluminum foil, the hut with pine needles, the starry sky made
with pins. But I would get bored arranging the characters, all
those little shepherds, busy people, shopkeepers selling their
fish, laundry women rubbing clothes against their washboards,
little peasant women with their baskets of honey, bagpipers as
annoying as any mariachi band. They ruined everything with
their zeal, uselessly busy in a landscape that asked for nothing
more than to be contemplated.

Digging furiously, my girlfriend was just as zealous. I was
trying to figure out how to take the shovel from her when we

saw some living creatures peer out of the ground. Or rather, one of the creatures was no longer living; my girlfriend had just sliced the body of an animal in half. It looked like a huge mouse, probably a mole, or whatever being might be hiding in the Miden underground. It was hard to make out the blood in all that dirt; it seemed almost like a magician's execution: two perfect halves of a body bereft of all humors. But around those two lumps there were little living creatures, a litter of the animal's newborn pups.

My girlfriend dropped the shovel and burst into tears. "What did I do?"

The creatures emitted no sound, maybe because they were too little or were mute. It was hard even to make out their gazes, those half-closed eyes like button slits. They had soft, slimy still-unformed bodies covered with a substance similar to mucus. You can't say they aroused feelings of tenderness—more like gentle revulsion. My girlfriend wouldn't stop crying.

"It wasn't your fault," I told her, even though that was a lie. Because yes, it was her fault. She'd scythed clean through the body of an animal and left its babies to wriggle in desperation.

She leaned over to get a look at the spectacle up close, extended a hand out to the little animals, and then recoiled. She couldn't bring herself to touch them. A sweet expression came to her face as she tried again to approach the slimy bodies, but her hand wouldn't move a millimeter. So she turned all her sweetness on me.

"We can put them in the suitcase and bring them home," she suggested.

"I don't think they make good pets."

"You'll be carrying your sarcasm to your grave."

It wasn't the worst thing I'd be taking to my grave, but this time I wasn't trying to be sarcastic. I imagined they were underground creatures, unable to survive in a house, especially deprived of whoever brought them into the world. Not to mention the fact that we had gone into the forest to bury a suitcase and would instead come back with a suitcase full of life. What sense was there in prolonging the agony? My girlfriend took the shovel again and tried to gather the pups together along with some earth and spread them into the suitcase. Her hands were shaking. When one of the animals was grazed by the shovel, it convulsed with agitation, and she jumped back with a shriek. The forest muffled nothing. I began to fear that the group of professional screamers might descend on us at any moment.

"C'mon, let's go," I said.

She became very serious.

"You're abandoning our child to wheeze in the mud."

At that point I became serious too.

"Okay, if this stuff is our child, why are you too disgusted to even touch it?"

Her seriousness segued into fatalism, then blame.

"Why didn't you take the shovel out of my hands?"

I much prefer insults to recriminations, but it seems that I inspire only the latter. At that point, though, I took the shovel from her hands, and she didn't put up any resistance. She leaned over again to the anguished creatures. She put out her arm till her finger was a few inches from their bodies. She forced a smile, the way you do in front of a patently ugly baby in a carriage. She stayed there for a few seconds, her arm extended and her finger wagging, her smile a kind of facial paralysis. She lightly brushed one of the little beings, and in response it tried to climb the mountain of her shoe. She shrieked again and jumped to her feet, shaking her shoe hysterically. "I can't take it! I can't take it—" She started crying again. I felt the threat of the screamers looming. The silence of the forest worried me more than her tears. I didn't know how they would react to the extermination of those moles, and above all I didn't want to have to justify the presence of that roller suitcase.

"I'll never be able to forgive myself," my girlfriend said.

Before she could stop me—and I don't even know if she really would have—I squashed the creatures under the heel of my shoe. They didn't crunch. Not even their death made a noise. I removed the scraps of their bodies from the sole of my shoe with a stick; then, with the shovel, I made a small pile of that organic mass and tossed it into the hole she had dug.

# Her

It dawned on me that what the girl had felt was similar to what I experienced in the forest: she may not have heard the blow, but the echo wouldn't give her peace. She had woken up one morning under the impassible Miden sky and an image came from her memory to disintegrate everything she thought she loved. I suspected that the whole process of raising awareness outlined by the Commission had to spring from a specific memory that would slip out of the file: a high-fever illumination, a distorted drawing on the wall, I don't know. Perhaps that memory hadn't even been mentioned, perhaps it was a secret she kept within her, just as I would keep the secret of the forest massacre. I was complicit. When she came to the house that day, I took her gaze as an accusation, a sophisticated artifice of hostility, which I tried to reflect back at her. Now I wondered whether it was *my* gaze upon opening the door that had dictated the rules of the encounter, whether *I* was the hostile one from the beginning. She seemed smug, distant. It hadn't occurred to me that she may simply have been uncomfortable. We both were. It must not have been easy for her to enter our house. I'd set up my tea ceremony in order to study her. Who knows, maybe she would have preferred a beer. I didn't even ask her. I imposed the slow torture of tea on her, watering down the tension with boredom, like in a meditation course. After she told me she'd been raped, I rushed to put on some music. I couldn't figure out the motives behind my gestures. I didn't trust her, and I didn't trust myself.

In the questionnaire, they asked me if I had ever been subjected to violence by my boyfriend. He didn't want to read my answers when the questionnaires came back. Part of me was grateful because I was disappointed with my answers and I thought he would be able to tell, my sentences rolling like marbles, then petering out. But I also felt humiliated. He knew writing was my ambition, and in the past his attempts at encouragement—like anyone else's—made me even stiffer, more fearful. People still think that having talent is better than having none, but I've never seen any proof of that. I told myself that one day, when everyone stopped spurring me on, I might be able to put something together. That day never came, but I didn't wait for it any more than I would wait for happy hour to have a drink. I remember a whole afternoon as a teenager spent burning myself under the sun because I was unable to dive. I knew how to swim, but the idea of leaping from a rock paralyzed me. There was no other way to get into the water. Everyone urged me to jump, adults and friends, they held my hand or made a playful gesture to dive in, but all I felt was my skin searing and the terror of jumping. "There are jellyfish," I said. And fortunately, there were jellyfish, but it was a lame excuse considering that even children climbed and dived from the rock, swimming amid the little jellyfish in the water.

I always looked for jellyfish in my life and always found them. I realized how ridiculous it was to consider that questionnaire a test of my writerly ambitions, but that's how I felt, and even my boyfriend knew. That's why he decided not to read it, though he said it was a form of respect, which made it even more humiliating, an exemplary punishment. I wondered if he behaved that way with his students too, if he avoided judging an assignment when he assumed that it wouldn't be up to his expectations. I couldn't imagine him as a strict professor, nor could I imagine him as a kindly, affectionate man. Surely he had his strategies for not hurting his students' feelings, but I hated it when he used that same measured condescension on me. In any case, when I was asked if I had ever been subjected to violence by my boyfriend, I said no. All I wrote—all I *claimed*—was that we'd had violent sex. The claim had nothing to do with consensuality; it was about narcissism. I wanted to make it known that we fucked well. That I was satisfied. That my boyfriend made me come. That I knew how to reach an orgasm. That was my talent! I didn't think the question could refer to other forms of violence. Why should it? I had a kind man beside me. The same man who had squashed those newborn creatures in cold blood. I had proof that could alter the verdict. I felt powerful with that explosive in my hands, so powerful as to be vile. It meant bearing witness to my faults as well: the fatal blow of the spade, my inability to hold a shovel, or to respond to simple but embarrassing questions. What exactly were we doing in the forest? We were there to pollute the Miden soil. We were there to hide my inadequacy. We made things worse, like an oil stain that spreads as you try to clean it. My mother always used some such example. Or maybe it wasn't oil, it was milk. Whatever, that was the sense. The problem was me. The problem was getting all the way to Miden with that roller suitcase, the problem was leaving my country to meet a man, any man. The problem was spending entire days preparing tea. The best thing I did in those last days was to scream in the middle of the forest.

# Him

I was sorry to leave behind the cradle I'd built, partly because I knew I'd never build another one. The cradle I'd used as a baby was still in my parents' basement. First it had belonged to my cousin; then it was passed on to me and finally to my brother. "Don't make them like they used to . . ." my father would say. I couldn't argue with him. That unassuming cradle had survived the restless nights of at least three kids and was ready to welcome new generations. It was more than just good craftsmanship or durable materials, it was about objects created to last through time, with no pretense of being remembered. The way it passed from hand to hand created simple bonds, a sharing without the urge to possess. We're always obsessed by the idea that someone can take our place. Wouldn't it be much easier to think about human relations in the same way? For example, in one photo I'm in the cradle, in another photo my brother is. Neither one of us would want to be in a photo hugging a woman if she had already been hugging the other in a previous photo. Likewise, no woman I have ever been with would be happy to see me at ease in the arms of another. What a pity. In any event, I thought about how happy my parents would be to exhume the cradle in the basement. They would exchange one of those knowing smiles capable of bringing a little spice back into a relationship. We did well to hold on to that thing, they would say. And I, who had built a cradle with my own hands, wouldn't be able to enjoy my son's admiration when he reached the age to become aware of what his father had done. Just the thought of it made me nervous. I felt judged by a person who in most respects was still not a person. I would have liked to tear that yellow cradle apart with the same fervor I'd built it. Or maybe my son would grow up ignoring his father for years, just as I'd ignored mine. Then one day the thought of his father would come back to betray him, like an unassuming serpent slithering into his mind. He would think about foolish things, about the little magazines his father had bought him after school, the meat juice he'd made for him when he had a fever. I don't know why, but my father was convinced it could cure all childhood ailments. He had faith in iron and believed that distilled meat would make me a stronger man. The memory of the juice came back to me in a moment of weakness, and I called him to ask how to make it. Instead of curing myself, I prepared the meat concoction

for my girlfriend. When she allowed me to take care of her, I
felt like a better man. My father spent all his life taking care of
his family, preserving that cradle in the basement, treating it
against termites and airing out the space. I would have liked
for my son, years from now and far away, to think of me in
the same way. I would have liked to see him smile, his heart
full of gratitude. I would have liked to hear his hesitant voice
asking me for the meat juice recipe.

# Her

My boyfriend bought me a nice sporty backpack, one you could travel the world with. But I was just going back home. We hadn't thought about what to tell people back in our country. Usually you'd go home only if a parent was ill, and even then people look at you suspiciously; they welcome you but smell the odor of defeat. Our defeat—if you want to call it that—would also give us some satisfaction. When we had the courage to tell the whole story, there would be material for many evenings. It was the perfect tale for entertaining people; there was room for moral intervention, which would invite people to give their opinion: If I were you . . . But that's absurd . . . In my book . . . They could identify bloodlessly with the lives of others. Then someone would take me aside and ask: So how are you?

I thought about how I would react to hearing our story as an outside observer. What would I have thought about the girl? Well, she's a girl . . . What would I have thought about myself and my angry indolence? My time wasted. Hours spent at home. The grimaces of boredom. The inane rituals: tea, the market, walks on the beach. I wasn't a very likable person, never mind charming. Even the ghosts that haunted me were piddling little animals.

*So how are you?*

*You have a sad look in your eyes.*

*You look beautiful, but you have a sad look in your eyes.*

I'd decided to wear that look, and I wasn't beautiful. One morning, in a fit of madness, I covered all the mirrors in the house. By that point my boyfriend would let me do anything. She'll get over it, I heard him say in his head. Maybe he'd read some of the manuals—prepartum depression wasn't so rare. The book would advise some sort of remedy, and he'd surprise me, buy me fish and grill it in the yard. Cleaning up was a drag, and I didn't lift a finger. He chose that beautiful backpack. In order to shave, he had to pull aside a sheet draped over the mirror, but he did it without complaint. Then he put it back over the mirror. I wanted to fuck, but my body didn't react. I told myself it was because of those animals buried in the earth. But I didn't tell him.

*So how are you?*

I'd written to my mother to let her know about my return.

"What great news!" she said. "We're so happy."

"You're supposed to say *I'm* so happy, Mom."

"I don't understand. How long are you staying?"

"I don't know, Mom. Why not enjoy the good news?"

I could hear it from a distance, her terror.

"I never get to see you."

I'd covered the camera on the computer with a piece of tape. I told her it was broken.

# Him

When I started to empty the drawers, I reconsidered the girl's dirty panties I'd kept for months. It seemed absurd that I could have done something like that. If my girlfriend was nearby, I'd close the drawer quickly, afraid that the smell might contaminate the air between us. Up until that moment I hadn't yet realized the degree to which rationality had long abandoned us, how all our actions were nothing but responses to the fear of contagion. She wandered around the house like a black ghost, convinced that her body was getting wider every second. She harnessed herself under a sheet that had a hole for her head. When she went out, she wore a raincoat over the sheet. But she rarely went out, only to go for a walk on the beach, and she came back with the edges of the sheet soaked with water and sand. She even asked me to prepare her things, to fill her backpack with what would fit. She didn't care about what was left out. When I tried to get her to participate, she swaddled herself under that ratty mantle and stared at me, expressionless. She watched me without saying anything as I folded the little blouses that wouldn't fit anymore and slipped them into the backpack. There was a sweater of hers that I'd never liked much, a long, gray, professorly cardigan. "Should I leave it out?" I asked her. Total silence. Then she came up to me and pounced on the cardigan, as if I were a baby and she had to free me from a rabid mastiff. She tried to tear the cardigan to pieces, which wasn't easy with just her bare hands and no scissors. All she could do was stretch it out, use her teeth to tear the yarn, then throw it to the ground, exhausted. I picked it up because I suddenly found that woolen heap endearing.

"I begged you not to ask me anything," she said. "But you just can't help it, you're still looking for approval. Why don't you do what you want and leave me in peace? I don't want to decide anything, okay?"

"I thought we'd decided together to go away."

She looked at me as if the words had come to her several minutes ago, and she was unnerved by their useless echo. The room seemed colonized by our words. They rooted themselves in the furniture, climbed up the walls, and her silence was a fragile screen, just like that sheet she wore.

"If yes, then how do you judge this decision?" she said scornfully. Then she conceded a smile. "Okay, let's say that's how it is. We made this great decision together, but I don't want to decide anything anymore. So go finish packing and stop hassling me."

She sank into the couch, and the black sheet slid like a graceful wave revealing her nude body. She tried to calm the wave and cover herself again in a hurry.

"I don't want to leave in these conditions," I said.

"What would those conditions be? They're kicking you out of here. I don't know if you understand. You're no longer the one dictating the conditions."

"I'm talking about us two, not the others."

She burst out laughing.

"And who would the others be? Do you want to make war with the whole world? Have you thought about when we return? The others will be waiting for us. There will always be others. What's your plan? Do you think we'll always be holding hands and playing footsie under the table? Is that your idea? There they are, they're coming. Look at how beautiful they are! A parade of faces all curious about our arrival. The peanut gallery getting together to tell us how good we were together. What elegance, look at her dress! You putting your hand on my bare neck . . . Me tilting my head toward your shoulder. Is that how you imagine it? Do you think anyone will give a shit about us? Just us two? 'I'm so proud of my boyfriend!' No, maybe at that point you'll be my husband, sounds better, no? 'I'm so proud of my husband!' You'll have your little story to tell, for a while it'll keep you at the center of attention, so take good care of it. Maybe it will help you pick up another girl. And then that, too, will end. And the girl will find someone else more interesting. And we'll both be parents, and our child will be someone else too. So I don't know what you're talking about. Enjoy this novelty for as long as it lasts. They're kicking you out of here, they won't do it again."

I smiled at her. More silence.

"And you?" I finally asked.

"And me what?"

"You're not being kicked out of here."

"I know. It's frustrating. I should have thought about it first, but by now . . . all I did was kill an animal in the woods."

"I'm afraid that's not enough."

"No, that's not enough. And I buried a roller suitcase."

"Not enough."

"I'm too pregnant and depressed to think about seducing a young guy."

"You want to seduce me?"

"I couldn't handle it now."

"But do you want to leave with me?"

"I don't want anything anymore."

"That's fine. So have you decided to leave with me?"

"Yeah, okay, yeah."

"And you'll help me pack?"

"No."

# Her

At four in the morning I slid out of bed because I couldn't sleep. The house was shadowed by a grayish, uncertain darkness. Little birds were already awake, busy with their morning song. The scent of a new season came in through the window with the insistence of someone who considers himself welcome until proven otherwise. I closed the window: that was the proof otherwise. The luggage left half packed in the living room reminded me of when I arrived. There was even more disorder now, like the mess of an adolescent slacker committed only to fucking all day. There were clothes scattered on the floor, little accumulations of sand carried back from the beach, books piled on top of each other as they waited for a final destination. It didn't look to me like a house that was alive, not even when I first set foot in it. It was welcoming, according to the Miden directives, but now even the sense of hospitality

seemed corrupted, like a nice tablecloth that reveals a pattern
of stains from meals consumed in solitude. I would wake up
in the middle of the night with hunger pangs after dreaming
that I'd taken a bite out of a whale calf. In the dream I had no
compassion for the calf. It was an ugly animal, deformed, with
hard, hostile skin; taking a bite out of it not only sated my onei-
ric appetite, but even proved my vigor. The fridge contained
nothing like whale meat, so I made myself a sad sandwich
with cheese and greenhouse lettuce, then wandered around
the house. In one of the last questionnaires to arrive, my boyfriend's hairstylist—who was also mine—described me as an
introverted woman when it came to her own desires. Whereas
most people saw me as socially inept, he was one of the few to
articulate a deeper understanding about my personality. He
could describe in minute detail my hesitation—or rather, my
"ambiguity"—every time I went for a haircut. He said I always
came with a photo; then I would listen with scant conviction
to his advice and stare at myself in the mirror as he proceeded
to cut. I'd limit my reaction to grimaces of impatience, after
which I would remove the towel from my shoulders and run
away from the shop with my hair wet, before he could blow-
dry it, pretending I was satisfied and making any excuse to
get away as soon as possible. The hairstylist admitted that he'd
never managed to conform to the photo, he'd never managed
to establish enough trust with me to get me to open up, to
discover my *real* (italics are his) desires with regard to how

I saw myself in the photo of another. He didn't consider me socially inept as much as a person incapable of accessing her *real* desires and just as incapable of communicating them, so I wound up presenting the image of someone else ("the photo of a woman with a stylish cut") in order not to reveal myself. I would never have imagined such attention on his part, and I appreciated it, even though his observations weren't complimentary. What he wrote was true. I knew the anxiety of the hairstylist's chair well, looking at myself in the mirror in a paradoxical effort to not look at myself, to dim the lights so I wouldn't have to confront whatever figure might be blossoming in the reflection. I wouldn't have known how to judge it, wouldn't even have wanted to. My sense of dissatisfaction in that chair was always too tenacious, and I needed it, I was terrified by the prospect of looking at myself and being content with my image, reconciled with that image. Those were my *real* desires, to always keep their fulfillment at a distance, so far away that the desires themselves stopped taking shape.

It might seem strange to say it, but I felt too fulfilled in Miden. As I walked around the room, I thought about everything that had seemed only a mirage inside the tent that long gone summer: learning another language, living together, leaving my country. I felt as if I'd stopped falling short. I was learning another language, living with my boyfriend. I'd left my country. I was even expecting a child. I could start fantasizing about his future, and one day even that would fulfill me.

It wasn't important that I'd turned over the responsibility of packing the bags to my boyfriend; at some point they would be ready, I would hoist the backpack over my shoulder, head for the airport, take a plane, and return. My anxiety in the hairstylist's chair, that loneliness of mine, would have worn thin. I would have felt lonely all the same, dissatisfied with myself, but in a different way. The house's shadow reminded me of everything I would no longer be, the grayish darkness of indecision, night's threshold, with the birds already awake.

# Him

The loudspeakers started blasting the sound of barking dogs. My girlfriend and I had forgotten about the drill. She was underneath me, biting her hand like she was about to have an orgasm. She didn't always do this, only if she was about to have a particularly intense orgasm and was trying to get the most pleasure out of the sense of anticipation. Or at least that's what I thought. It's not easy to gauge another person's pleasure from the outside. Not easy, but gratifying. That night, however, I knew she was biting her hand because the tension was real, a turbulence that made us vulnerable, plundering each other's bodies as if conquering territory. It was unexpected sex. She woke me up and held my arm tight ("It's the part of you I like best," she said to me in the beginning. "You're objectifying me," I responded), and she looked at me with free and sincere abandon.

When the barking dogs started, we both burst out laughing. The tension was transformed into a sweet release, a gentle mist of unexpressed pleasure.

"Fuck, they're right to throw you out of here," she told me, joking. "You can't even remember the basic rules . . ."

The basic rules called for remembering the earthquake drills, but in any case she had forgotten them too. The barking dogs went on for a few minutes, so we put on our underwear. She took my T-shirt and went to crouch under the table.

"And me?" I asked.

"Stay bare-chested, I want to look at you."

I obeyed. We stayed under the table simulating a fear we had to control, the way they taught us in training. My girlfriend started licking my neck.

"You can't do that," I said.

"I'm doing it," she said, and kept licking me. I slipped my hand into her panties. She was still wet.

It was strangely exciting to think of the Miden inhabitants crouched under tables, waiting for the second alarm. It seemed impossible that they were all following the security instructions, but even my girlfriend and I hunkered down under the table, both of us simmering to some extent. I imagined a far-off orgy, lots of people who would copulate at X hour, expansive moans together with the recorded sounds of dogs. Actually, the best idea was that of an orgy that didn't foresee copulation, only the increase of excitement in anticipation of an alarm that would never come. Endless moans under all of Miden's tables. Forever. And no one to watch, no one to control, only the imaginary divinity who had choreographed that nocturnal earthquake drill so he could see his devoted herd panting with pleasure. I was elaborating my cosmic desire for crouching men and women when it suddenly occurred to me that there should also be children. The fantasy rapidly dissolved. To compensate, I felt my girlfriend's pussy getting wet on my fingers, and my dick regaining its splendid erection. I moved her head closer to my dick, and she began sucking it. Then she sat up with a start.

"Are you afraid, my love?" she asked.

"Be quiet and keep going." She went back down on my cock, and the second alarm sounded. She bit my arm and ran outside. I lost some seconds looking for another T-shirt while the alarm grew louder and louder. I was also looking for a pair of pants to cover my erection, but someone knocked at the door, kindly reminding me that my life was in danger. Fortunately, the T-shirt was long enough.

When I went outside, there were a bunch of people in the streets. Children were running around, having fun, as if they had all been looking forward to waking up in the middle of the night for an earthquake drill. They were used to that kind of exercise during the day, at school, but in the dark it was an adventure. They moved frenetically through the street, their suitcases ready, eager to show their parents how independent they could be—men and women in miniature who simulated our own simulated feelings: anxiety, fear, solidarity. There were helpers who handed out coffee in thermoses, and a coordinator who updated us on the next steps. But in reality we didn't have to do much except wait for the alarm to die down, so all the coordinator did was calm us down with his mellow radio voice. My girlfriend and I were the only ones in our underwear. It was cold. She started shivering next to me, embarrassed by her nudity. A little girl put her suitcase on the ground (we had even forgotten to take our emergency luggage—which everyone was required to have ready in case of emergency, but the fact was that our emergency luggage had been taken apart to pack bags for our departure) and took off her red windbreaker. She hesitated for a few seconds, unsure whether to wait for a sign of approval from her mother, then decided it was time for an adult decision. She approached my girlfriend.

"For the boy, or girl," she said, trying to position the red jacket over my girlfriend's belly.

# Her

The verdict came in the midst of a beautiful storm. My boy-friend and I had opened the envelope over breakfast. We weren't surprised. He was the Perpetrator. I was his partner. He had two weeks to leave Miden, his expenses covered by the community. But the courtesy was wasted, we'd already bought our tickets. We'd be leaving in five days. I'd read the weather forecast. The storm would last till the following day, then the weather would be overcast but without any showers, and we would leave Miden under relatively clear skies. We took everything out of the fridge. My boyfriend cooked omelets and served them on a tray with fluorescent strawberries. He went to make coffee. We opened the windows wide to let the rain in. The mug fell from my hands due to what I could only describe as a perfect unhappiness.

# Him

Anguish can resemble calm, a terror so fatal that you appear serene to those beside you, a dead and peaceful man. I couldn't feel my heartbeat when I opened the envelope with the verdict. I couldn't feel my breath. Sure, I was expecting that outcome. Rationally, statistically. I was expecting it up until a second before, an instant before, an infinitesimal that slackens time into an era before the Word. Then came the words. When I read the words, I felt my heart beating again and my heavy morning breath. I abandoned my mineral state. I was able to ingest nutritive substances. I smiled at my girlfriend. "I'm a Perpetrator," I said.

I looked for an object to hurl against the wall, but my urge was weak. I flipped the porcupine sculpture over; it fell to the floor and a few quills broke off. My girlfriend leaned over to gather them and pricked her finger.

Other words came to me in those days. Telephone calls from those who had voted against my expulsion, people who vented with me and considered the verdict a glitch in the system. They expressed indignation and trust in me. You can have another trial, they told me. They elaborated strategies for the near future, a future that would reach me in absentia. I listened to everything. I nodded. My voice was calm. I was a calm man. The Miden sky began to clear after the storm.

I thought of passing by the Academy to say goodbye to my students, but I didn't want them to feel uncomfortable. I fantasized film scenarios, a heroic welcome, a revolt in the name of the professor who fell from another world. But I'd never been that way. I was a professor like many. I had only done my duty, then made a mistake. At that point I hoped that they would quickly forget me, that I would stay with them like an autumn from their youth. The memory of a strange November, not much more. And only now that my status had passed from professor to Perpetrator did I realize that language created reality. I was inside that reality. I had raped a girl. I had loved a girl and raped her. Until that moment I didn't even consider it a possibility. All the anger of the last days slid away, all the rage that had kept me alive. I was a calm man. I was a man so calm I was finally dead.

# Her

We left Miden on a day perfect for arriving. The sky's lumines-
cence glared like the overexposed background of a photo; my
boyfriend's profile stood out against it like a bird in flight—a
clear-cut sign that marked the presence of life in that divine
white. That's how creation must have been: the light bracing
itself with elements, a geometry taking shape. Then came the
gigantic quartzes, the monoliths of a cult we had taken too
lightly.

The wind from the open car window tousled my hair and I
thought of my gray strands, like fugitives discovered in their
shelter behind my ears. If my boyfriend had turned to me,
he would not have seen a girl with her hair in the wind, but a
woman going gray at his side. I squeezed his thigh tight at that
thought. He grabbed my wrist and hit the gas as if he wanted
to shorten the distance that separated us from the future.

Here we are.

Those were the words unuttered inside that car. The words unuttered for days. I put on sunglasses to protect myself against Miden's supernatural light.

"Does the wind bother you?" my boyfriend asked. "You want me to roll up the window?"

I smiled at him. It was no bother at all. It was pure, limpid air. Pure, limpid pain. With sunglasses it was more bearable. Things melded together; the gigantic quartzes became suffused with a pinkish patina, a clumsy color correction. I chose those glasses intentionally for their warm tones. They made the landscape look artificial, and I could bear the artificial. It was all I could still manage to bear. Soon I'd start dyeing my hair and the wind wouldn't reveal the gray of my age. These things reassured me, imagining other versions of myself. Going back to buying tight-fitting dresses again, dabbling with eye shadow, even foundation, me who never used makeup. I don't know, I'd make something up.

Here we are.

At the airport this time, I had a proper backpack, an enviable backpack. How beautiful! Where did you get it? they'd ask me when I got back. Eh, in Miden! But eventually the envy would die down. I've never been an envied woman, I don't have the right bearing. I didn't have my roller suitcase, so no one plugged their ears. No wheels, nothing to pull, only the sound of steps. A dignified thing.

Here we are.

There was a group of kids at the check-in. My boyfriend froze. They were there for him. They had come to say good-bye. I gave him a pat on the back. "Isn't that nice?" I said. And there I was again, envying someone. He was so caught up in the emotion that he didn't answer. He was happy in his embarrassment, a little boy who sees a pussy for the first time. "That was nice, wasn't it?" I insisted. My boyfriend seemed bothered by my maternal tone. "Yeah . . . yeah," he muttered. I felt that my presence was making him nervous. I could un-derstand. He never let me participate in his relationships with his students, but the Miden community certainly did, in the most violent way possible. Maybe part of his discretion was the fruit of my apparent lack of interest. I never asked him questions about his lessons, I mixed up the kids' names and faces, I tended to dismiss his anxieties about giving a lower grade than he would have liked. One time he wouldn't touch any food because of that anxiety, and that night he couldn't fall asleep. We wound up fighting, probably because I was too sleepy to indulge his torments. When I had the chance to take part in an event organized by the Academy, I stayed in a corner, bored, drinking goblets of bad wine and looking at the young girls' muscular calves. Some of the male students were fun, a few of them I would have taken to bed with me. That was the most I'd confided to my boyfriend. Little quips about me, about him. Homespun orgy fantasies. I never took his role as

professor too seriously. Or maybe I took it so seriously that I
felt inhibited, excluded from everything that had to do with
his academic life. I felt sorry in that moment. I thought back
to the argument when I kicked him out of bed just so I could
sleep. That was long before I became an insomniac. I could still
apologize. I could still become a better girlfriend, a better wife.
The idea of having to remedy something consoled me, moored
me. I could return to my country with good intentions. What
I could never fix were my failings with respect to Miden. The
orange poncho abandoned on the floor of the house, the creatures buried underground with the roller suitcase, the missed
appointment with the Organic Pesticides Commission. Feeling
continually uprooted had absolved me on many occasions. I
thought of the past solely to glorify my sense of exile. I didn't
know if I would feel like an exile back in my own country. I
knew that the poncho, the moles, and the organic pesticides
were only a pretext, because there was something much graver
for which I couldn't manage to forgive myself: my hatred for
the girl. I could become a better girlfriend, but life would never
give me any respite from that hatred. That feeling was still
there, intact, till the end; the girl had turned me into a rapist's
girlfriend. We started walking toward the check-in where the
students were, and I took my boyfriend by the hand, felt him
recoil from my grip. He turned toward me. "You want to go
ahead?" he asked. "I'll say goodbye to them, then join you . . ."

# Him

The flight landed thirty-seven minutes late. I noticed because I was thirty-seven years old. I think that's when my madness started; once the first coincidence was established, everything became a sign. The airport in our country had gained a considerable reputation for dysfunctionality; political battles were fought over the issue. How could the contemporary world accept us with such a shoddy visiting card. It was an area that lent itself well to rhetoric. It allowed for the conjugation of a social ideal with more seductive abstractions: imagining the future, migratory flows, the need to empower the proliferation of non-places. I think there were further cuts and layoffs after the Crash, but on the day of my arrival, the absence of personnel was offset by the absence of travelers. The half-deserted airport highlighted every gesture of those who were there. I sensed that I wasn't the only one to seem busier than necessary, unscrewing water bottle caps, rolling cigarettes to smoke out-side, tying shoelaces tighter, checking the conveyer belt display with the absorbed gaze of someone reading a newspaper who is aware of being observed. My flight's luggage was on conveyor belt number nine. Another unequivocal sign. It was the same number as the row of my seat on the airplane. The bags were strangely on time. It was the first time that had happened to me at that airport. I couldn't express my unspeakable surprise because my mind was engaged in a further thought: How should I interpret the brevity of that wait—or rather, the total absence of any wait—between the landing and the activation of the conveyor belt? Were they keeping me from thinking? Were they deliberately subtracting the time I would have to formulate hypotheses? The signs multiplied; the meanings became more obscure. Surely it could not have been chance— the fact that my bag was the first to come out while my girl-friend's bag was the last. I felt sorry, and she would have felt sorry too, because when her backpack was finally spat out of the conveyor belt's mouth, there was no one to admire it. Her beautiful, compact, essential backpack. The backpack I had prepared for her, carefully choosing the clothes I wanted to see her wearing, the books I wanted her to read, the cap with the pom-pom meant to embody our future melancholy. The backpack made its solitary and circular journey, then returned to the mouth, came back out, then in and out again. Who knows if she had pictured this scene. I suspected she'd planned it, and a part of me applauded her theatrical flair. Making the decision after checking in her luggage, leaving me there to watch the perpetual motion of her backpack on the conveyor belt. I was practically alone in front of an Uroboros. It was a sight even more powerful than her empty seat on the airplane. I yelled like a madman when the flight attendant with her practiced gestures closed the plane's hatch. "There's a passenger missing!" "Calm down, sir." "Open the fucking plane!" "Sir, please sit down. We are about to take off." Two people escorted me back to my seat. Very softly, thoughtfully. "Sir, please sit down and fasten your seat belt."

The other passengers started to get agitated. They were tourists; my face didn't mean anything to them. I was just some crazy person on their flight. They may have been worried about violence, but they couldn't imagine what I had left behind.

"Let me off!" I shouted, grabbing one of the attendants. One young man unfastened his belt to intervene. The attendant gestured for him to go back to his seat. She never lost her smile. Not even when her lips came close to my ear, her breath fresh from a just-sucked mint. "I'm sorry, you can't get off. You are no longer welcome in Miden."

# Her

I cut my hair very short. It's electric blue. I'd dreamt of blue hair ever since I was a teenager, but adolescent rebellion had taken a less extroverted form: silent quarantine. Blue suits me even now.

My baby was born. It's a girl. I thought till the end that it would be a boy.

"She has her father's mouth," the others tell me with a hint of sadness. But I'm not sad to hear it. Her father has a beautiful mouth. I miss his lips. I sent him photos of his daughter. My Rolleiflex left with him, but they gave me another camera as a gift. They told me my photos were beautiful. They tell me a lot of nice things. I know he gets the photos, but he doesn't respond. I'll keep sending them, though. I still don't feel like sending him a video of our little girl. Even if I kept myself out of the frame, a certain amount of interaction would still be noticeable. My girl would react to my prompts. Who knows if she can already perceive the blue of my hair. I don't want to alter their relationship, I don't want my presence to arouse resentment in her father.

The girl comes to see me often. She takes care of my daughter if I want to go out. But on some afternoons all three of us stay at home. I've stopped making tea. When she came to see me the first time, as soon as I got out of the clinic, she asked me what the baby's name was. I hadn't decided yet.

"Give her my name," she said.

"Why not?"